W9-BFI-040

The BEADED MOCCASINS

The Story of Mary Campbell

by Lynda Durrant

A YEARLING BOOK

Published by
Dell Yearling
an imprint of
Random House Children's Books
a division of Random House, Inc.
1540 Broadway
New York, New York 10036

ISBN: 0-440-41591-8

Reprinted by arrangement with Clarion Books

Printed in the United States of America

November 2000

10 9 8 7 6 5 4

OPM

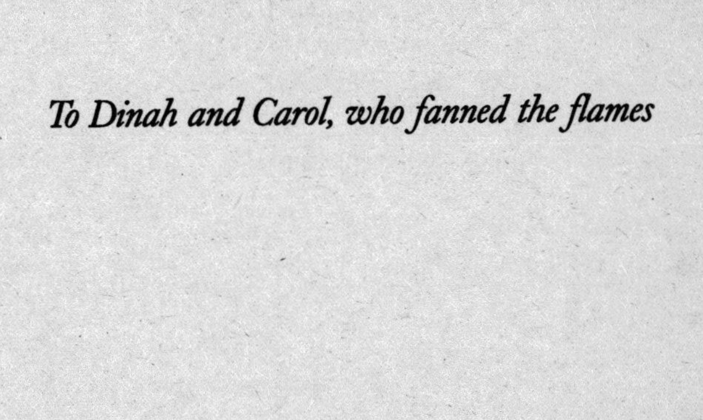

To Dinah and Carol, who fanned the flames

Contents

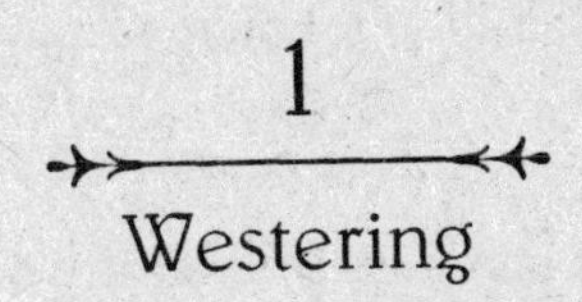

1
Westering

"MARY CAROLINE CAMPBELL, that's no way to card wool." My mother takes the carding boards from my hands. "Watch me again."

I sigh my very best martyr's sigh. We are sitting by the fireplace on a beautiful morning in May. Gray barn kittens practice their pouncing on my bare feet. They bite, scratch, and kick while their mother stretches in comfort by the fire.

"Ow! Lady Grey," I say sharply, "take your kittens back to the barn, please." But she just closes her eyes and pretends she can't hear me. I sigh again.

A kitten has climbed into the wool basket and it overturns, spilling raw fleece onto the floor. A draft catches bits of wool in a tumbling dance, and the kittens give chase. One catches a bit of fluff in her teeth; the fuzzy wool gets into her nose and makes her sneeze. I get up to pull the fleece out of her mouth. More bits of wool drift across the floor, and the kittens pounce on them as though they were tiny mice.

The front door is open to let in light and fresh air. A green mist of tiny spring leaves covers the trees that remain on our claim. Our sweet-smelling fields are still moist from the April showers.

"Mary. *Mary.* Sit down. You're not even paying attention."

"I'm watching."

The carding boards are made of wood with slender, sharp nails poking out in even rows on one side. My mother takes them in her hands again. She places a lump of raw wool on one of the boards, seizes the handles, and pulls one board against the other. The impurities (the dirt, sheep dung, and twigs) that were bound up in the fleece fall to the earthen floor. She pulls and pulls until the lump of raw wool has combed clean into thin, even threads.

"Now you try, Mary dear."

She watches me carefully whilst I pull and pull at a lump of wool. Dirt and dried sheep dung fall as a powder into my lap. The only good thing about wool carding is the lanolin, in my opinion. That's the oil on the fleece. My hands and forearms will ache tonight, but they'll feel as soft as a princess's after carding wool all day.

Even so, carding wool is the last thing I want to do. "I want to go outside," I complain, "into the lovely May. Tomorrow's my birthday. It's not to be borne."

My mother's mouth is a tight, thin line–a line I've

seen before. "Mary, dear, who's going to card and spin the thread for this year's clothes? Your brother has outgrown everything he owns."

"Dougal can card his own wool," I grumble, just loud enough for her to hear me.

The winter has been a hard one, and I have a most direful case of spring fever. I ache to be outside; my blood feels just like the sap in the trees, all restless and rising.

A column of sunlight filled with dust motes shines through the cabin window, the motes floating gently through the air. Dougal is reading out loud from our Bible. His feet are as restless as a colt's as he stumbles badly over the words. Just as I do, he glances out of doors every chance he gets.

"Matthew Five: 'And the multiply . . . the multi*tude* . . . came to hear the serpent on the mount.'"

I laugh so hard, I drop my carding boards. "The serpent on the mount," I shriek. "The *serpent* on the mount!" Kittens scatter like frightened birds.

Dougal's jaw is set as hard as a horseshoe. "There *was* a serpent," he says stubbornly. "It says so right here."

"Dougal, dear, surely that isn't right," my mother says gently. "There was a serpent in Eden with Adam and Eve. I think you mean the Sermon on the Mount."

Dougal squirms on his bench.

"What did the serpent say?" I shout from the fireplace. "Tell us what the serpent said!"

Dougal grumbles, "I don't care an owl's hoot about reading and figuring. I want to go outside and find more arrowheads."

"Dougal, dear, that's enough. You're fourteen; you should have learned to read years ago."

"I can read–just not the hard words."

She hesitates. "Wait for your father to come back from plowing. He'll help you."

"So I can leave now?" Dougal snatches up his musket and lunges for the door.

"No, dear," she says firmly. She gets up, seizes Dougal's musket, and puts it on the mantelpiece. "Read until your father returns. Copy the words you don't understand."

"Awww," Dougal mutters. "I don't know them. I'll learn 'em wrong. That's worse than not learning 'em at all."

"But Dougal–" My mother falters.

"No!" I shout. "It's not to be borne!"

"We'll read tonight," Dougal says quickly. "We'll study together, Pa 'n' me."

Dougal and I wait, holding our breaths. Dougal is hunched like a wildcat, ready to spring.

"All right, Dougal dear," my mother says. "As long as you promise to read tonight with your father."

Dougal fetches up his musket from the mantelpiece. "Thank you! Thank you!" He gives her a big kiss and races out the door before she has a chance to change her mind.

"That boy!" My mother shakes her head, but her face is lit up in pleasure. She's never looked at me that way. I hear him clumping down the porch steps.

Now it's my turn. "I can card the wool tonight too. We can card together."

"No, we can't," my mother snaps back. "We'll be spinning tonight. You need the sunlight now, to card out the impurities in the wool."

"But Dougal has your leave. Why must I remain and breathe impurities?"

Mother ducks her head and smiles. "Dougal needs to practice hunting, Mary. He's working, just like you."

"He's not working," I say bitterly. "He's outside sporting." We can hear him crashing through the underbrush, whooping and hollering like an Indian.

"Not another word."

"But–"

"Men have their work, and we have ours. The two seldom meet."

"He's not working," I mutter under my breath. "You know he's not working." My mother pretends she can't hear me.

"I hate Pennsylvania," I say with a stamp of my foot. A kitten has curled herself around my instep. She growls and bites my ankle in retaliation.

I scream, "Blood! She's drawn blood!"

"Mary," my mother says sharply. "You're much too young to be so hateful. All you have to show for it is a sore ankle and a vexed spirit. Not another word. We've carded enough wool for a bit of spinning. That's a welcome change."

I walk stiff-legged to the spinning wheel, growling kittens clamped fiercely to my ankles. I pull them off like burrs.

I plump down on the spinning-wheel seat just as hard as I can, hoping it will break. It doesn't. I thread the wheel faster than a pig eats a piecrust, heave another sigh, and set to.

My right foot stamps the pedal and sets the spinning wheel into a whirling blur. As the wool ravels in, my mind ravels out.

Cumberland, Pennsylvania, is beautiful and wild, but I was born in a proper town–Fairfield, Connecticut–a stone's throw from Long Island Sound. Fairfield's clapboard houses crowded around the town square so prettily, like dinner guests in their Sunday best around a table. There were two churches, with steeples poking into the sky like candlesticks.

There were tea shops and bakeries. Two drapers offered the best fabrics from England and France. Our next-door neighbor was Fairfield's only dressmaker and a wondrous gossip.

Now instead of gossip we hear wildcats screaming in the night. Instead of pretty houses we see bear tracks round our door in the morning.

Dougal loves living in the western wilderness. Once he came back from the woods too excited even to speak. His hands were full of arrowheads. Not five years ago Indians lived where our cabin stands today.

Stamp, stamp, stamp, my foot pounds the spinning-wheel pedal.

I look up, startled to see my mother watching me from across the cabin. Her mouth is a tight, thin line again.

"I want to go home," I say softly.

"This is your home. Home is your family."

"But Connecticut–"

"We're a westering family, Mary dear," my mother says firmly. "You're to make the best of it."

Westering. How I hate that word. More than a year ago I'd seen the westering look on my father's face. He had that restless, dreamy gaze in his eyes and that stubbornness round his mouth as he watched the sun set beyond our town.

I cried myself to sleep that night because I'd seen that look on plenty of menfolk's faces already. That look meant sobbing on the shoulders of girl friends and then watching their families leave Fairfield for the western frontier. Christmas last, I heard my father say in a low voice to my mother, "Elizabeth, good land to be had in central Pennsylvania, now that it's safe."

So a year ago March first it was the Campbells piling our belongings onto an overloaded wagon and saying good-bye. At the Crown's land office in Philadelphia my father laid claim to four hundred acres of land along the Susquehanna River.

All he had to do was show a profit in five years' time and the four hundred acres would be his. But the river bottomlands were clogged with oaks, the roots clinging willfully into the earth. He said some of those oaks were two hundred fifty years old, maybe older. Perchance that's why the roots were so stubborn about letting go. It took my father, Dougal, and our neighbor, Mr. Stewart, one month to cut the trees down. They tore the trunks out with our yoked oxen; the roots they dug out with felling axes and their bare hands.

And why were the Campbells cutting down oaks that

had been mere saplings at the time of Columbus? To grow pumpkins and corn.

I remember thinking: Where will the birds build their nests? But my father looked so proud, talking about turning the wilderness into a proper plantation, that I kept my thoughts to myself.

Three days later the fence was finished–pig tight, horse high, and bull strong. Our cabin was next, then the barn. The cabin is less than half the size of our Connecticut house. My room was on the second floor with a window facing the bright blue of the Sound. We had oak-planked floors instead of just packed earth. And rugs.

I sigh again.

We card and spin all day, stopping for a quick repast of tea and corn bread as the shadows lengthen against the eastern wall.

I lay the carding boards in the near-empty wool basket. My hands ache, my neck has a crick in it, my eyes sting. Lady Grey has taken her kittens outside.

"I need to go outside after our tea," I say in my best ladylike voice, "into the woods. If only for a moment."

"All right, Mary, return in a moment."

As I dash for the door, my mother moves toward the fireplace. Usually I help with supper. I tell myself not to think about her, cooped up in the house all day and now with a meal to prepare all by herself.

Freedom! I walk into the pasture, drinking in the cool air of late afternoon as though it were icehouse cider.

This year's pasture is a good ten acres. Next spring my father and Dougal will cut down another ten acres for the spring lambs and calves. They'll clear-cut ten again, and ten again, year after year.

Patches of wild strawberries grow amid the timothy and clover. I must remember to pick some.

Dougal is sitting on a rock in the middle of the pasture. Penn's Creek, which we named for William Penn, winds its way around the rock and toward the Susquehanna.

"Mary, look at this," he calls to me.

He unrolls a parchment map onto his lap. As I study it, the cattle and sheep gather round for a closer look.

"Go on, git." Dougal throws creek pebbles at the livestock, who gather up their clumsy dignity and scatter. "Durn cows, git.

"Look, Mary." Dougal points to the map. "This is Lake Huron, one of those great lakes in the French claim. And this is the Ohio River, and here's where the Ohio empties into the Mississippi River. Way out west, that's the Missouri River. That's where I aim to go, be a trapper along the Mississippi and the Missouri rivers. Folks say there're places along the Mississippi where it's seven miles wide. You can't even see the other side. On the Missouri the beaver are as big as those sheep."

"But that's French land," I say to him. "French and Spanish. They argue over the Mississippi and Missouri rivers all the time."

"Who cares about them? The Mississippi's so big, they won't even notice."

"They'll notice if you can't speak French or Spanish."

Dougal studies the map intently, tracing the river systems with his index finger. But I know he's trying to think of a reply.

Finally he does. "I'll pretend I can't talk."

"Can't talk?"

"I was crossing the mountains and the biggest snake in the world attacked me. No one knows about the snake because no one has ever been in those mountains before except me? And he was going for my neck, but I turned just in time and he bit me right on the tongue so now I can't talk. A western mountain snake–I'll be known as the Silent Trapper."

I can't resist. "And which mountain snake is that–the serpent on the mount?"

"Awww."

I study the map. The solid black lines that mean rivers dip and curve like purple martins flying after mosquitoes. Near the French and Spanish rivers are little drawings of bald monks, Indians with tomahawks and canoes, buffalo, bears, wildcats, deer, and herds of wild horses. Thicker lines lie next to them. The short, thick lines follow the twists and turns the river lines take. I know these short lines are the names of the rivers. I know they're letters strung together to make words.

"What does this one say?" I point to another river line.

"Susquehanna," Dougal says importantly. "That's our river, right here in Pennsylvania. See?" He traces the river line with his finger. "But the trapping's no good here anymore. The Susquehanna's trapped out. Pennsylvania's good for nothing but farming now."

"How do you know the Mississippi isn't trapped out?"

"Because it isn't, Mary!" he says impatiently. "And even if it is, I'll just find another river even farther west. There must be hundreds of rivers out west. I'll ask when I get there."

"The Silent Trapper asking about rivers?"

He rolls up the map. "Why am I wasting my time talking to a girl? Girls wouldn't give a pig's eye for westering."

"Westering." I spit the word out like a rotten berry. "This is what you've been doing all day, isn't it? Hiding in the woods and mooning over this map. You're so lazy."

"No, I haven't." But Dougal won't meet my eyes, so I know I've guessed the truth.

Westering means fresh starts and new beginnings. Any problem can be solved by heading west, any itch can be scratched by heading west. At least that's what menfolk think.

My grandfather must have had that same restless, dreamy look in his eyes when he tore my grandmother away from Scotland to sail west across the Atlantic to the colonies.

What if my father gets that look in his eyes again? I imagine him marching across this very map with Dougal and my grandfather in his wake–west through the French lands, then west again to the Spanish lands of papist California. Finally, there the Campbell men stand on the edge of the Pacific, their pant cuffs wet, scowling at the ocean because there's no more west to go to.

Mission monks raise a rumpus and try to shoo the Campbell men away with the hems of their black robes, now wet and rimed salt white from the ocean waves.

I laugh, and Dougal looks at me curiously.

"What's so funny?" he asks.

"California."

"California rivers," Dougal exclaims. He leans closer and studies the western edge of the map.

"I want to go to Mrs. Appleby's Dame School," I say in a small voice. I have never said this out loud before. "Do you remember my best friend, Constance Farnsworth? We were going to start school together. I want to leave Pennsylvania and go home. I want to live with Grandfather in his pretty house on the town square.

"And when I grow up, I want to live in a real house with flower gardens and a second floor and lace table-cloths and napkins and polished furniture and a staircase and neighbors who shout 'Good morning' from their side of the fence. I want to learn to read and write and ride in a two-horse carriage to church and have elegant tea parties in the afternoons."

Dougal snorts. "Girls."

The black river lines get bigger; they blur and fill in with water.

"Don't cry, Mary. You'll see Connecticut again someday."

"No I won't," I sob bitterly. "I'll never see Connecticut again, Dougal."

When Dougal and my father are snoring in their beds, I lie awake. Farthest from the fireplace, my bed and I are hidden within deep shadows. Every night since the end of April, I have stayed awake, watching my mother sit by the fire and stitch my birthday dress.

I lie absolutely motionless, scarcely breathing, because she'd say, "Hush, Mary dear, and go to sleep" if she knew I was watching. The half-moon curve of her face, arms, and hands is lit up by the firelight.

Before we left Connecticut, she packed away a bolt of bright-blue cloth, the same color as my eyes. So close to the coals, the blue cloth glows almost pink.

She puts the dress down in her lap and rubs her eyes. Suddenly she looks tired and sad. My mother has many friends in Fairfield. Her sister lives there, too, my clever and funny Aunt Orpah, whom we may never see again.

"Hush, Mary dear, and go to sleep."

"I didn't say anything."

"Hush now."

As I roll over, I wonder, How did she know I was awake?

2

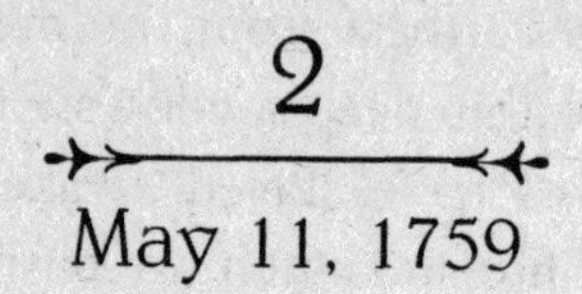

May 11, 1759

IT'S MY BIRTHDAY, but I don't *feel* twelve. I roll over in bed and wait for any change. No, I still feel like eleven.

I turn my head to the sound of my father's feet touching the floor. It's almost dawn and he's going to our neighbors' farm a good two miles upriver. The Stewarts are a young couple with a two-year-old named Sammy. Mr. Stewart and my father are going deer hunting together.

My father shuffles around the cabin, stubbing his toes on bench legs and knocking his knees on barrels, cursing under his breath. I want to ask him when he'll be back, just to see if he'll wish me a happy birthday. But he's in such a foul temper that I stay hushed.

When he opens the door, a slice of lemon-yellow dawn lights up his profile. And then he's gone.

Soon after, my mother staggers in from the barn with

a bucket of new milk in each hand. She's always the last one to retire at night and the first one to awaken in the morning. Ma sets the kettle on for tea and places corn bread on the table.

"Mary, it's daybreak."

It's light enough now to see my brand-new birthday dress draped across the chair back–with a lacy, store-bought chemise on the seat. I slip the chemise and dress over my head, and they fit perfectly. I tie my lace collar, the one from Flanders, around my neck. As I whirl around, pretending to be surprised, I admire the deep flounce of the skirt. I lift the hem and see a bit of frothy lace at my calf.

"Oh, they're beautiful. Thank you, thank you, thank you!"

My mother wags her finger at me. "You knew all about this dress, young lady. You've been watching me when you should be asleep. But I've managed to salvage a few surprises for you."

"The chemise is a surprise. It's from Fairfield?"

"It's from Paris."

I am flummoxed. "France?" Never have I had anything so elegant and pretty. Or expensive.

My mother's mouth is a tight, thin line again, but her eyes are twinkling. "So you were surprised. You're becoming a young lady. Young ladies need pretty things." She points to the table.

At my place is a birthday cake. I smell cinnamon, maple syrup, and the dried apples my mother brought all the way from Fairfield.

"It smells delicious."

She cuts a huge slice of birthday cake and places it in a napkin. "Cake for breakfast?" I ask.

"Surprise."

I sit in our front yard and take huge, un-young-lady-like bites of cake. Tiny white violets have filled in the nooks and crannies between the grass blades like a slight spring snowfall. When the sun comes up red over the Susquehanna, it tints the white violets a deep, glowing pink.

Sunlight dapples the wavelets as though someone had scattered gold coins across the river.

What would I do with those gold coins? I'd spend them on dolls more beautiful than princesses. I'd buy delicate china cups and saucers for tea parties. I'd have more candy than at a dozen Christmases, more fancy clothes than in a queen's closet.

My bare feet are cold against the earth, but the spring sunshine glows warm on my face and hands. I remind myself sternly that eleven is much too old to be this excited about a birthday.

And yet . . . the air is soft, my dress is new, my chemise is from Paris, my lips still taste of cinnamon. This is my day–fresh, young, and full of promise.

A *thunk* on the side porch makes me turn my head. My mother is heaving the butter churn onto the rough-hewn planks.

"Mary, take off that new dress and put on your old brown one. The butterfat will ruin it."

I stare at her in horror. "But this is my birthday–"

"Yes, but milk won't churn itself, especially once the sun gets hot. Hurry, or all we'll have is cream for your labors. You'll want butter for your birthday dinner, won't you?"

I sit on the side porch in the shade, punching the churn stick up and down, up and down, in the butter churn. Already my shoulders hurt and I'm hot and sweaty. My sunbonnet is no relief.

Dougal isn't even awake yet. He's here to protect us, and his lazy tail isn't even out of bed yet! Of course he's peevish because he's not deer hunting with the men.

"Not so hard at first, Mary dear. You'll slosh the milk right out of the churn. As the milk turns to butter, you'll be thankful you saved your strength."

Even my eyes are hot, I'm so angry. "Why does Dougal get to lie abed?" I shout. "It's not to be borne!"

"You'll be sorry you wore that new dress, young lady."

I shove the churn stick down hard, and sure enough, milk leaps out of the churn and splatters onto the porch and my new dress. Lady Grey, her kittens, and a mob of other barn cats gather round to share in the bounty.

"Mary," my mother says, "your father and I were up before dawn. He so you'll have meat on your plate; and I so you'll have milk for your tea. We all work very hard."

"And Dougal?"

"You leave Dougal to me. Churning, candlemaking, wool carding and spinning, weaving and sewing, cooking, sweeping, washing and cleaning, preserving, and taking care of children: That is what young ladies need to learn to do. You'll get married someday, and your husband will expect you to do them all."

"I already know how to do them all!" I shout.

"Hush up," Dougal mutters from his bed.

"You hush up, Silent Trapper!" I scream so loud my throat feels like bursting.

An even larger crescent of barn cats is at my feet, licking more milk that has sloshed out of the churn. I see my life in front of me: an endless round of churning, carding, spinning, weaving, sewing, cooking, cleaning, childbirthing and rearing, and following a westering husband even farther away from Connecticut.

I scream, "I don't care if we don't have butter!"

I fling the stick and churn cap out into the side yard. The cats crouch low but still lick up the milk, faster now. They watch me with wary yellow eyes, ready to spring out of my way.

"I can't be like you," I shout. "You can't even read and you live in a one-room cabin in the wilderness. I can't grow up to be you–I'll die!"

Her face turns as white as the milk; her hands fly to her cheeks as though I've slapped her.

We stare at each other for a moment.

"I can't be like you," I repeat through clenched teeth. "You're like one of our cows: dim, dull, and stupid. And you've always loved Dougal more than me."

She just stares.

Strawberries, I think, my heart in my throat.

I run in the front door as Dougal rolls over in bed.

"Where do you think you're going? And where's my breakfast?"

"The pasture," I whisper fiercely. I pull the hair at the top of his head and pretend to scalp him. "Where the Indians are. Get your own breakfast."

His eyes widen. "What Indians?"

"You're so stupid!" I scream at him. "You're the stupidest boy who ever lived!"

I snatch the rose bowl from the table and run outdoors.

My mother is picking up the churn stick as I run past. Waves of barn cats jump from my path like the parting of the Red Sea.

I don't even look at her as I jump over the fence and run to the pasture.

It's a beautiful spring day. The sort of day when I can imagine the blue, green, and golden days extending forward forever.

Our five cattle and the three sheep stand around in a dumb-as-dirt clump, the cows chewing their cuds. As I pant for breath, the livestock gaze at me blankly. One by one they return to grazing. With their noses and hoofs they crush the strawberries, filling the air with a delicately sweet tang.

The sun is already hot. I remove my sunbonnet and lift my long hair; the breeze off the river is delightfully cool against my neck.

The wild strawberries cover the back side of the pasture, which is so far from our cabin that all I can see of it is smoke rolling lazily from the chimney.

The wild strawberries are tiny and pungent–their taste explodes in my mouth like a musket firing. In no time my tongue feels burny and sour from the juice. The jagged strawberry leaves grow close to the earth, and the tiny berries hide underneath them as shy as deer. I stay close to the ground, crawling along on my hands and knees (watching out for cow pies, of course).

A slice of birthday cake, no matter how huge, is no proper breakfast; I'm so hungry, I eat half the berries I pick.

The rose bowl came all the way from Scotland. My grandmother gave it to my mother the day Dougal was born. The bowl has red roses and dark-green leaves painted in the bottom. Strawberries fill the bowl to the ends of the roses. The tips of the painted leaves are still showing. The delicious smell, the sunshine, and the thought of strawberries with fresh cream for our pudding make my mouth water.

I'll give my mother the strawberries, I decide. That will make her happy. She'll forget all about the fight.

We'll have wild strawberries and cream with our midday meal. That's even better than butter. I'll give her strawberries in the pretty rose bowl. The cream will have risen to the top of the churn by my return. She'll have fresh cream, wild strawberries, and an "I'm sorry" whispered in her ear.

Anyway, there would be days and days like this one to come. "Strawberry summer days," I say out loud. My tongue is still burning from all the berries I have eaten. "Not blueberry days, not peach days, not apple days. Strawberry summer days."

Still famished, I eat a lot more berries. Too late, I notice the strawberry stains down the front of my new dress.

The breeze off the river dies, the trees, the birds, even time itself seem to stand perfectly still.

An odd-shaped shadow splays in front of me–a many-headed darkness with shadow feathers sticking out around the top. Cooler air sets me to shivering. The hair on the back of my neck stands up even as my heart starts to pound. Why? Has a cloud blocked the sun? No. But the shadow . . . the feathers . . . a dreadful feeling that I'm no longer alone.

My father's livestock bolt away. I hear someone gasp "Mary!" I whirl around.

Four Indians in war paint and feathers. Flies buzz around fresh scalps hanging from their belts. The Indians have a stillness to them, as though they're saving their strength.

When I stand up, one of them takes the rose bowl from my hands.

"Oh, Mary," Mrs. Stewart cries out. Her face is chalk white with terror. Two-year-old Sammy Stewart is in her arms, stirring in his sleep.

"We walk," one of the Indians says calmly.

They're dressed in breechcloths and deerskin leggings. Braided hair hangs all the way down their backs. Red paint covers their faces and chests, tattoos swirl over their arms and legs. Copper and silver earrings hang to their shoulders.

"We just came from our farm," Mrs. Stewart cries out. "Our farm in flames! And Mr. Stewart away deer hunting!"

She's right, I think. Deer hunting–my father won't be home until dark.

I hear a roaring sound from the river. Smoke is billowing over the trees. My mother! My brother! Our cabin in flames! A fifth Indian runs across my father's pasture while the livestock trot clumsily out of his way.

"We walk," the first one says, urgently this time. He's older than the others, with iron-gray hair. I take a step backward and then another. I glance toward the forest.

All of them reach into their belts and take out their knives. They take them out slowly and with no malice, as though they just wanted to admire the bone handles or look at their reflections in the knife blades. As quick as smoke, two stand behind me.

"Mary, don't give them any trouble, please," Mrs. Stewart begs. "We'll be rescued. I know we will."

"My name is Mary Caroline Campbell. I live here. Th-this is our farm. I live here." If I could just explain, they might see their mistake. "My father claimed this land . . . in Philadelphia. And I was named after our late queen, Queen Caroline.

"This is Mrs. Stewart and Sammy." Mrs. Stewart half drops into a curtsy, then freezes. She pulls herself upright and holds Sammy closer to her.

"We walk, Mary Caroline Campbell, named after your queen," says the older one. I notice he didn't say "our queen."

I look toward the pasture gate. The cattle are there, waiting. Our bull looks at me in mild surprise. The four cows crop grass again. Sheep run around in circles, bleating in slack-jawed sheep panic. Our chimney falls through the burning roof with a crash.

"We walk," the older one repeats.

For once, that fussy crybaby Sammy isn't crying. He's staring at them wide-eyed with his hands stuffed into his mouth. Only then do I notice that Mrs. Stewart's hands are bound together with grapevine rope. She's struggling to hold Sammy against her.

"We walk, Mary Caroline Campbell. Now."

I pick up my sunbonnet and tie the strings under my chin with trembling fingers. The old one pulls more grapevine rope from his waist pouch, and they tie my hands together too.

I start to cry. "No, please no."

The grapevine rope smells of tobacco and digs into my wrists.

One of them gives me a shove toward the forest and we walk. Just like that, we walk.

We quicken our pace in the woods. We walk past the tree into which my father chopped a tomahawk improvement to mark the end of Campbell Station. We trot over a stream, then double back; we splash over another stream and double back again. We cross and crisscross valleys and hollows, we run up ridges and passes. Between sobs I remember every crisscross and gulley, I memorize every streambed. The older man peers deeply into my face every hour or so.

By nightfall we have been running every which way and I have no idea where we are. I feel hollow with hunger and thirst and jumpy with terror. I'm exhausted, too, and hot. I can't stop panting for breath. Nothing looks familiar. I don't even know which direction I'm facing.

The old one, the one who spoke English, holds my face by the chin and looks deeply into my eyes, as though trying to gaze into my thoughts.

He does the same thing to Mrs. Stewart. Finally, he nods and speaks to the others. They stop immediately and clear a space for a camp. They use flint and brown pine needles to start a fire.

"Sit down," he says gently. Mrs. Stewart and I fall to the ground just like the walls of Jericho.

"Please, sir," I start to sob. "Please, I want to go home." Little Sammy Stewart hears me crying and commences wailing too.

"I have been watching your face, your eyes," the old one says. "Once you were sure you could find your way back, and now you are not sure. And home is far away, to the west. I have never been there, but we have heard it's a good place. The British have ordered us to go west."

"West! No! It's . . . But it's my birthday." As soon as I say it, I know how ridiculous that sounds.

"Food." The old one gives me a handful of samp–that is, cornmeal–and a drink of water from my grandmother's rose bowl. What happened to all the strawberries I picked?

One of them cuts away the rope binding our hands.

The old one says, "Food and sleep."

The next morning I know I've been dreaming about Fairfield, because I can almost smell it. The spicy-sweet scent of the bakeries makes my mouth water. The bready aroma of the alehouses fills my nose. I smell the molten iron from the blacksmiths' shops; a whiff of lye soap from Monday washdays almost makes me sneeze. I shut my eyes tightly, hoping I'll go back to sleep and dream more. But then I hear Mrs. Stewart moaning as she awakens. I see the five men kicking dirt into the fire to ruin evidence of our having been here. Fairfield disappears with the sunrise. It was safe there. The Indians were long gone.

Sammy Stewart refuses to eat the wet cornmeal they have given us for breakfast. Mrs. Stewart holds the meal up to his face and he shouts, "No!" with a turn of his head. "No!

"Wan' milk," he says.

"There's no milk, my darling." She holds the meal out again.

"No!"

The men pull on their knapsacks. As we commence to march, Mrs. Stewart staggers under Sammy's weight. He tries to wriggle out of her grasp and cries and cries.

Late in the morning I see a bluebird singing in a little oak tree. His bright-blue feathers are the same color as my dress and eyes. His silvery, liquid voice fills my ears with a promise: I will see my family again.

At evening the old one says something, and the others stop immediately and start a fire.

Mrs. Stewart drops Sammy to his feet. The two of them walk to a nearby creek, and she washes him and his pants.

We gather around the fire as the forest fills with darkness and mosquitoes. We eat the same thing meal after meal: cornmeal mixed with water. It always seems as though a few handfuls of samp won't be enough, but when I drink more water, it swells up in my stomach.

Even Sammy eats tonight.

I'm surprised to be so grateful for little things: sitting down at last; cold water to drink; a full stomach; I will be sleeping (and dreaming) soon. As I lie down, the forest floor feels smooth under my back. Another thing to be grateful for. Last night tree roots poked into my back till morning.

Now I can tell them apart. The old one who speaks English is their leader. The tall one always walks or sits next to him. He must speak English, too, because I know he understands what I say. The two younger ones must be brothers, they look so much alike. The fifth one has smallpox scars all over his face and body.

I doze off to sleep to the buzzing of insects. "Escape," they whisper into my ears. "Escape, escape."

I dream again but not of Fairfield. I'm at Campbell Station, sitting with my family around the hearthstones.

"Escape," the fire hisses into my ears, "escape, escape."

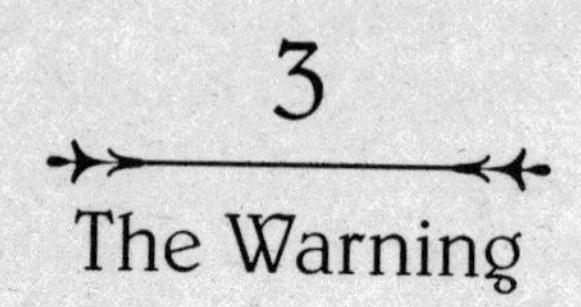

3
The Warning

SAMMY CRIES AND CRIES, and I spend half the night tossing and turning. The next morning he drinks so much water, I think he'll burst. Mrs. Stewart's eyes are as red as her dress, and there are dark circles above her wan cheeks. When she tries to give Sammy wet cornmeal, he smacks her hand away with another "No!" The Indians stare as the samp splatters into a poison ivy patch. They glare at Sammy. Mrs. Stewart groans as she picks him up.

"Please God," she says softly, cradling Sammy's butter-bright blond head. "Please give me the strength I need today."

I say, "I'll carry him, Mrs. Stewart."

"No, Mary. You need your strength."

The Indians stamp out the fire while Mrs. Stewart hoists Sammy onto her back. She grasps his ankles, Sammy puts his arms around her neck, and we commence to march again.

Sammy whimpers a bit, then falls asleep. He must feel like dead weight on her back. His wrists must be choking her. Stooped over, Mrs. Stewart falls farther and farther behind.

It's close to noon, I reckon, and steaming hot. We are scrabbling up a steep gorge. I see a flash of Mrs. Stewart's red dress far below us.

The Indians start talking, but of course I have no idea what they're saying. The old one, the leader, says something to the big one with the smallpox scars. We stop and wait for Mrs. Stewart to catch up.

Smallpox Scars holds out his arms.

"Thank you, sir," Mrs. Stewart says wearily. Sammy tumbles, still asleep, into his arms.

Smallpox Scars takes Sammy behind a tree.

"Where are you taking him?" Mrs. Stewart calls out. She begins to follow, but the tall one holds her arm.

Smallpox Scars comes back with a scalp of baby-fine yellow hair covered in blood.

I cover my mouth to keep from shrieking.

"God in Heaven, no!" Mrs. Stewart screams when she sees the scalp. She pounds on the chest of Sammy's murderer, but Smallpox Scars just stands there stone-faced. Mrs. Stewart might as well beat on a tree trunk for all the good it does her. She collapses onto the forest floor, beats the ground with her fists, and screams and screams.

They wait patiently for her to stop. Her screams turn to moans, then sobs. Finally, Mrs. Stewart rolls into a silent ball.

"We walk," the old one says softly.

I kneel next to her and touch her arm. "Mrs. Stewart, please," I whisper. "Please don't give them any trouble." But Mrs. Stewart closes her eyes and pretends she can't hear me, the way Lady Grey did when I complained about her kittens.

The tall one lifts her to her feet.

"We walk," the old one repeats.

"I'd rather die," she croaks.

"Then die."

They pivot on their feet and walk away, the old one pushing me in front of him.

"Mrs. Stewart," I shriek. "Please don't leave me." Which sounds peculiar because I'm leaving her.

We commence to march again. I'm crying so hard, I can't see in front of me–I stumble and fall over logs and roots.

After what seems like a long time, she catches up and slips her hand in mine. "I'll never leave you," she whispers. We link arms and walk. Mrs. Stewart's hands are coated with loamy earth.

She buried Sammy, then caught up with us.

I am hungry, thirsty, footsore, heartsore, and so tired and terrified that I can't think straight. But I don't say a word. Smallpox Scars is walking ahead of me, and when I look at Sammy's tiny scalp woven into his long black braids as a decoration, and a warning, I don't dare complain about anything.

Mrs. Stewart stumbles forward in a daze, hour after hour, day after day. When she looks at the scrap of scalp, I'm not even sure she knows it's Sammy's anymore.

It must be June. We have been climbing mountains day after endless day for four or five weeks now, I reckon. Sometimes we spend an entire day climbing–winding our way around treefalls, pulling one another up the steepest parts, and thrashing through the underbrush–only to find that we've made little headway by dusk.

I thought we'd be marching next to the flat creekbeds and riverbanks, but the Indians ignore the water and study the sun instead. On occasion one of them will climb a tall tree, high above the other treetops, just to get a look at it. The creeks and rivers flow south. We're following the sun, heading due west.

We're crossing the Appalachians, I think with a lump in my throat. How will my father and brother ever find us?

My new dress is a dirty, pricker-torn rag. My mother worked so hard to make this dress! I watch her neat stitches in the hems and sleeves break and unravel one by one.

Mrs. Stewart slumps to the ground for our midday meal. I must say something to her to boost her courage. At first she was trying to cheer me, but now it's the other way around.

"Not quite so hot this morning," I whisper softly. They don't like us to talk together. Her dull eyes stare into space.

This afternoon I trip and fall over a tree root. The tall one picks me up as though I am no heavier than a barn cat. He steps on the skirt of my birthday dress, and it tears away from the back of the bodice. I feel like shriveling in embarrassment. He can see the back of my chemise as he walks behind me! But they don't even wear underwear. The five of them don't even notice.

The heat today is fierce. Before we stop for our cornmeal-and-water supper, the old one points to a creek.

"You and your friend wash here, Mary."

To be polite, I reckon, the Indians walk downstream, with their backs turned to us, every time we bathe.

"Mrs. Stewart," I whisper as we stand knee deep in the cool water, "I've been thinking. Do you think the reason we haven't been rescued is because they killed everyone else before capturing us?"

"Nonsense, Mary," Mrs. Stewart whispers back as she pulls her dress over her head. "My husband and your father were away deer hunting."

"What if they killed them in the woods? And what about my mother? My brother, Dougal?"

"Everyone's fine," she says firmly. "Mary, you must gather your courage and ask the old one. He's taken quite a shine to you. But I'm sure they're fine."

"What if Lady Grey and her kittens are all alone in the wilderness, and the other barn cats, too?" I feel worse about my family, of course, but it's the thought of Lady Grey's family that makes me cry.

"Everyone's fine, Mary. Cats are very resourceful, nine lives and all that. The woods are full of mice and chipmunks."

"Lady Grey must wonder where I am. What if she was hurt and her kittens are starving? I used to play with them every day," I sob. "She was so proud of her kittens. She wouldn't let anyone else pet them, just me."

"Mary." Mrs. Stewart takes a deep breath. "Surely you would recognize the hair of your parents and brother. Surely you've studied the . . . remains slung through their belts?"

"If our folks were killed, they'd have their scalps. Is that what you mean, Mrs. Stewart?"

My brother has reddish-brown hair like mine. Both my parents are long since gray. And Mr. Stewart has hair as red as a new penny. All the scalps slung through their belts are black.

"They're taking scalps because of the war with France," Mrs. Stewart says grimly. "At least we're not French."

"But what about Sammy?" My question hangs in the air like the steamy summer heat.

I dry my eyes. Mrs. Stewart flails her dress across the water.

"They didn't kill our livestock," I say hopefully.

We stop in the evening to eat more samp. It must be July, I tell myself. It's so hot and muggy, it's like breathing into a singing teakettle.

The underbrush tangles around my ankles. Pricker bushes and stinging nettles hurt my legs. I look longingly at their leather leggings. A pretty birthday dress is no match for leggings.

I sit next to the old one. I take a deep breath and,

before I lose my courage, I ask him, "Who are you? I mean, what kind of Indians are you?"

He looks at me and smiles. "Unami. Part of the Delaware."

"Delaware!" I scream. "Delaware!"

My father used to say they're the worst, the worst of the lot. Worse than the Iroquois, even worse than the Shawnee. Once the Delaware lived along the Atlantic Ocean, as far north as New York, as far south as Virginia. But one hundred fifty years of warfare with us have turned the Delaware into pitiless murderers.

"Please sir," I cry. Mrs. Stewart pats my hand. The Indians sit in a circle, waiting for me to finish crying. And finish I will, of course; no one can cry forever.

"I won't breathe a word, on my honor," I sob. "I'll say I got l-lost in the w-wilderness. I won't say anything about you if you'll just take me home."

As I weep and wail, the forest around us becomes quieter and quieter. Maybe the birds and animals have never heard a person crying before.

The old one sits very still. He doesn't tell me to hush up; he sits and waits. Finally, I stop.

"You don't understand, Mary Caroline Campbell. You're to be given as a present to our king, our sachem, Netawatwees Sachem. His granddaughter has died. You will replace her."

He pulls samp out of his waist pouch. "We eat now."

"I want to go home," I say softly. No one even answers.

We are on the march again before I remember that I

was going to ask the old one if my family is still alive.

The next day one of the brothers has a deep cut in his foot, so we rest for the afternoon. The other brother strips a piece of bark off a willow tree and pounds the inner bark into a powder. He adds a bit of water to make a paste. His brother winces in pain as he lies down. He chews some of the paste and pulls a face.

"We have no cranberries," the old one tells me. "Cranberries are good medicine. Good medicine to eat, good medicine to use on the skin. Willow bark stops pain, but it does not help the healing."

I take a deep breath and my heart starts pounding. "What happened to my family?"

"They are well," he replies.

They are well.

". . . and are waiting for you on the banks of the Allegheny."

"No, the Campbells, I mean." I hold my breath.

"The Allegheny . . ."

"They were killed? You killed them?" I ask in a low voice.

"No." He looks at me coldly. "Your family is waiting."

Tonight they smear something greasy on my face, neck, ears, and arms. Clouds of mosquitoes buzz around me but don't light. The grease must keep them away.

Why are there so many mosquitoes now? On this side of the mountains the earth is different–level, soft, and damp. Are we closer to the Allegheny? When will I see the Susquehanna again?

I lie awake and scold myself. *This is your fault, Mary. That rumpus on your birthday morning, that's why you're here now. These Delaware heard you shouting. How could you have been so stupid? Why were you all alone in the pasture? Why didn't you run?*

A tree root digs into the small of my back. Recriminations buzz stubbornly around and around my head for most of the night, just like the mosquitoes.

The next morning I awake to what feels like tree bark rubbing my cheek. It is the old one, touching my face with his rough palm.

"We walk after eating."

After a breakfast of cornmeal and water we're on the march again.

I can tell no British have ever lived in these woods. There are no farms, no roads, no inns, no taverns, no blacksmith shops. There are no fences. Just trees–as big around as fireplaces and taller than church steeples. The trees are so dense, we can't see the sun. We walk day after day in a greenish, leaf-cloyed haze. When it rains, I hear thunder rolling and crashing above us, but under our thick canopy of trees the rain is as gentle as mist.

And the animals! Bright birds fly from tree to tree, so far up they look like tiny wildflowers caught in the wind. Squirrels and chipmunks scold us from high in the treetops. Once we see a dozing bear with two cubs sleeping by her feet. Does and tiny fawns nip at the grass growing in the glades.

One day we see a fox with a stick in his mouth walk slowly into a creek. The brothers smile at each other and kneel behind a log to watch. The old one sees me frowning and explains softly, "He has tiny insects in his fur. Watch how a clever fox gets rid of them."

As the fox walks slowly into the water, I can see the fleas jump higher and higher onto his back. Finally his head is black with fleas, his eyes narrowed to slits because of the teeming insects. Now some of them are jumping onto the stick the fox has in his mouth. When the fox is entirely in the water with just his nose and teeth showing, and all the fleas are on the stick–he lets go of the stick! The flea-covered stick rushes downstream.

I swear the fox is laughing as he climbs out onto the bank. He shakes his fur, gives himself a few quick licks, and trots into the forest again.

Except for Mrs. Stewart, we all smile together. Even Smallpox Scars gives me a quick grin.

We march. At dusk we sit down to eat again.

"Tomorrow we'll be at our village," the old one announces. "Perhaps our sachem's granddaughter and Mrs. Stewart have to go into the creek to prepare for tomorrow."

He looks at me steadily.

"Oh," I say shortly. "Thank you."

Mrs. Stewart and I follow the creek downstream a bit to a deep pool and drape our ragged clothes on the bushes. We sit in the water and scrub our skin with sand and pebbles. I let the clean water run over my sweat-soaked hair.

My clothes are stiff with dried sweat and dirt. When

I step out of the creek, I dip my chemise and what is left of my dress into the current and put them on still wet. I find a calm pool the size of a soup crock and gently scrub my lace collar between my hands.

"Mrs. Stewart, the old one seems certain Netawatwees Sachem will want me as a granddaughter. Why? It's as though they went out looking for a granddaughter. I don't understand."

"I don't know, Mary. All I can think about is my little Sammy in heaven and my dear husband," she says sadly. She braids my long hair and ties the ends with strips of shredded hem.

I turn around to face her. "We could escape," I say softly.

Mrs. Stewart turns as white as a dogwood blossom. "Don't say that word ever again. They might understand your intentions."

"But–"

She takes my hand. "Honey, we'd be roasted alive at the stake if we're caught. Do you want that?"

All my life I've overheard adults whispering about the stake. Until now I'd always wondered why a captive would take such a foolish, deadly risk. Now I know.

"I want to go home."

"Compare the two evils, Mary–remain alive among them as a prisoner or die a cruel death if retaken. Which do you want?"

"I want to go home."

"If we can just wait until we're rescued–"

"Mrs. Stewart, I'll give you a signal." With the speed

of greased lightning, I give my left earlobe a tug with my right hand. "That means it's safe to try an escape."

"Oh, Mary–"

"Promise me you'll come with me. Promise me we'll try."

"I promise you I'll think about your intentions. That's the best I can do."

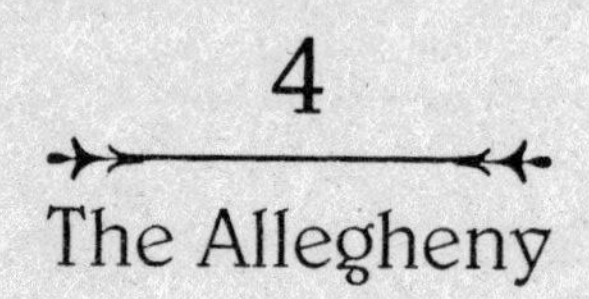

4

The Allegheny

LATE NEXT MORNING WE ARRIVE. We turn left at a huge buckeye tree, and I see twenty or twenty-five wigwams near a swift river. Women are washing bowls on the riverbank. A swarm of children are swimming close to shore.

Near the wigwams huge pots hang on tripods above cook fires. Hovering above the caldrons is steam so savory it makes my stomach hurt. I'm ravenously hungry for food, any food as long as it isn't samp.

"Allegheny?" I ask.

The old one nods.

Just then a tall, graceful woman holding two gourds steps out of a wigwam and comes toward us. "That's your mother, Hepte," the old one says. "Her name means Swan."

My mother?

The woman nods to us and gives the old one, then the tall one, each a gourd. The gourds are filled with water.

"This is your father, Coquetakeghton," the old one continues, pointing to the tall one. He drinks a little water from his gourd and gives it back. "In English his name is White Eyes."

That's easy, I think, looking at the tall one as if for the first time. White Eyes. But of course he's not really my father.

Women step away from the cook fires and come toward us. Several bring fragrant, steaming bowls of soup to the old one. I look hungrily at the soup bowls brimming with meat and vegetables. The old one sips a little soup from each bowl, smiles as he says something, and gives the bowl back.

"Netawatwees Sachem," one of the women says.

"You!" I shout. "You are Netawatwees Sachem?"

"Granddaughter." He gives me the same smile he gave to the women. "Welcome home."

Netawatwees Sachem's wigwam is bigger than the others. People crowd inside, their backs pressing against the bark-and-sapling walls, their faces lit up orange in the firelight. His daughter, Hepte, passes around bowls of soup to everyone. I reckon there must not be a Mrs. Netawatwees Sachem. Hepte gives Mrs. Stewart and me our bowls of soup last. As Hepte hands me my bowl, she says something to me in a soft voice.

I devour the soup. My grubby fingers slop steaming venison, carrots, and wild onions into my mouth as fast as they can. When I'm finished, Hepte gives me a bowlful of hot water and motions for me to wash my face with it. The wigwam, stuffed with sweating bodies, is stifling–but the hot water on my face feels like heaven. Mosquito grease melts off my face and hands like tallow off a rock in June.

As I wash, I hear them talking. The same words come up over and over. "Cuyahoga Sipi," "Tuscawaras Sipi," and "Oyo Hoking." Every time someone says "Oyo Hoking," they shout at each other, the women shouting just as loudly as the men. When Netawatwees Sachem speaks, the rest fall silent. He says "Oyo Hoking" more than anyone. They ignore Mrs. Stewart and me and talk far into the afternoon.

I nod off to sleep with the word "Oyo" in my ears. Someone lowers me to the ground and tucks a blanket around my shoulders.

The next day, for the first time since leaving Connecticut, I don't have anything to do. Mostly I stay in the wigwam, sleeping and hoping to dream of happier times in Fairfield. Instead, I dream of Campbell Station. I see my family sitting around the table, worrying me with questions: *"What's the date, Mary?" "What's the month?" "Why haven't you come back to us, Mary?"*

"Is it September?" I reply. They shake their heads sadly when my answer fails to satisfy.

"August?" I moan. "I don't know anymore–"

I awaken with a pounding heart.

Hepte's little daughter is sitting almost on top of me. She points at me and laughs.

"Go away," I say crossly. "Let me be."

She laughs again. While pointing to her heart, she jabbers something unpronounceable. I reckon she's trying to tell me her name.

"Leave me alone."

She laughs and leans closer.

I pull away, get up, and go outside to look for Mrs. Stewart. Hepte's daughter runs ahead of me. She jumps boldly from side to side, chattering while trying to snatch away my sunbonnet.

I point to a chickadee, perched not two feet away on a tree branch and scolding us brazenly.

"That's a chickadee." I point to Hepte's daughter. "You . . . a chickadee."

The little girl glows with delight. She twirls on her toes and to my astonishment does a perfect imitation of a chickadee's call.

"Chicka-dee-dee-dee. Chicka-dee-dee-dee."

"That's your name, then. Chickadee."

When I awaken a few mornings later, I'm looking at the sun. The wigwam is gone. Other wigwams are being folded up and lashed together with grapevines.

"You are awake," Netawatwees Sachem says softly. "We have been waiting for you to rest after our march. We are going into the Oyo Hoking. What the British call the Ohio Territory. They guarantee we will be safe there, and we have no choice but to believe them.

"We can live along the banks of the Tuscawaras Sipi

or the Cuyahoga Sipi. The Cuyahoga is farther away. We have decided to live there. Eat quickly. We leave now."

After a cornmeal-and-water breakfast, Hepte lashes a knapsack onto my back and gives me another pack to carry in my arms. My carry pack is heavy, with a rawhide strap that chafes the back of my neck. The contents shift when I squeeze it. I sneak a peek under the lid when no one is looking. The carry pack is filled with cornmeal. More cornmeal.

"You carry our family's food. An honor," Netawatwees Sachem explains.

I close the lid to the carry pack with a snap. That old Netawatwees Sachem doesn't miss a thing.

We follow the Allegheny south and ford at a wide and shallow place. I'm tired and my back already hurts from the knapsack.

Four days later we are at the forks of the Ohio River. I see Fort Pitt on the opposite shore standing proudly on the cliff far above: the Union Jack flapping in the breeze, the king's men in bright-red coats, the cannons pointing toward the river. I look eagerly at the ramshackle town of Pittsburgh, which has sprung up far below the cliff at the river's edge like a mess of skunk cabbage. My mother says Pittsburgh is full of drunken traders, even drunker Indian agents, and fancy women. But even the drunkest and fanciest would want to rescue me, I reckon. I decide to wave my sunbonnet in their direction.

Smallpox Scars stands in my path. He's blocking my view of the town and their view of me. His face is still but his eyes are full of murder. I turn away, my heart in my mouth.

At the top of the steep riverbank I look behind us to the east. Home. Family. A cabinful of problems left behind. Westering again.

We all stand on the riverbank looking backward. I see Netawatwees Sachem gazing at the fort, a look of dull defeat in his eyes.

"Oh!" I say, suddenly realizing something. The Campbells are westering because they *want* to. These Delaware are westering because they *have* to.

Someone steps on my birthday dress from behind and the last of the stitches around the waist give way. I step out of the skirt and just leave it. I don't even look back. They're all mostly naked anyway, their shining skin the color of russet potatoes.

It's been ten weeks (I reckon) since I saw my parents and my brother. What would they think if they saw me, trudging through the wilderness as burdened as an ox, wearing a battered sunbonnet, a delicate chemise from Paris, and grimy underdrawers?

I think about Columbus marching though the New World in his underwear, claiming every footstep for the King and Queen of Spain. When I laugh, Hepte looks at me and smiles.

As I lie on the forest floor this steamy evening, sweat drips down my forehead and trickles into my ears.

My father once told me that trees perspire, just like

people. He said a big oak tree will give off gallons and gallons of water in a day. The more leaves there are in a summer forest, the higher the humidity.

These massive trees make the air incredibly humid. I could gather the night air in and wring it dry like a dish-towel. I can't sleep. Why did Netawatwees Sachem wait to tell me who he was? Why didn't White Eyes tell me I was to be his daughter? I watch Smallpox Scars, the man who killed Sammy, singing to his children as they nod off to sleep. His ravaged face looks gentle, his eyes brimming with loving kindness.

When I figure it out, I feel chilled to the bone.

Netawatwees Sachem was watching me, deciding if I'd be a good granddaughter. If I hadn't pleased him, he would have told Smallpox Scars to kill me, too.

5

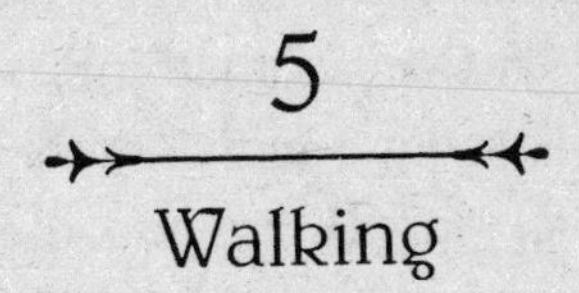

Walking

EVERYTHING HURTS.

My feet, my neck, my legs, my shoulders, even my elbows hurt. Even my fingers hurt.

We walk single file, with some of the men and boys walking ahead of and some behind the women and children.

My stomach growls all the time because there's never enough to eat. I'm always thirsty, even though I drink and drink at every stream and creek we cross. I splash water on my face, but still sweat drips down my forehead and stings my eyes all day.

In my mind's eye I see my mother's cooking, so real I can almost taste the juicy pork roast with plum sauce dribbling down my chin. The pastry surrounding her mile-high apple pie would melt in my mouth. Her cherry butter is tart and sweet, all at the same time. Her bread is as light as a cloud.

There are about two hundred of us, and each is carrying something. Even the younger children are carrying small covered baskets filled with dried berries and fruit. We don't walk very fast. The little ones walk for half the day. Then, after our midday meal, we have to carry them. So the second half of the day is even slower and harder than the first. We do stop as soon as evening falls because of them, so that's something.

Mrs. Stewart is staying with another family. At first she refused to carry anything, and the family's grandmother lashed a pack onto her back. It's tied behind so she can't take it off. I feel sorry for her; even the dogs are fed before she is.

Each midday we eat by a streambed. I've learned how to mix ground, parched acorn flour with deer fat and enough water to form a paste. We roast it wrapped around sticks. The mess tastes like burned wood. They gobble it down as if it were a Christmas goose.

I will never be like them, never! They're heathens without proper clothes or proper homes. They eat what animals would refuse. If Netawatwees Sachem thinks I'm going to be his granddaughter, he's in for a surprise.

But if I show any regret or rebellion or even sadness they might dispatch me just as they did baby Sammy.

So . . . I'll be as meek and mild as a newborn lamb, all the while hiding my real self. I'll be two people–the lamb the Delaware will see on the outside, and the real Mary on the inside. They'll never see the real Mary, never.

"That's what I'll do," I whisper to myself.

"You are smiling," Netawatwees Sachem says to me.

"It is a beautiful day." I give him my very best lamb smile.

"A beautiful day," he says, smiling back.

I almost bleat. It works!

This midday Chickadee has a bad cough and looks about as tired as I feel. She lies down on the forest floor and begins to whimper softly.

When we stand again, White Eyes picks up Chickadee and arranges her on his back. Her eyes have an empty, feverish look; her coppery skin is even redder than usual.

When I smile at her, Chickadee's face lights up as she smiles back. She reaches out and pats my face with her hot, chubby paw. I see Hepte's worry-clouded eyes as she tucks a blanket around her daughter's shoulders.

God causes the diseases that kill the Indians by the thousands. Just as in ancient days, when God took up an avenging sword and smote the Canaanites so the Children of Israel could enter the Promised Land, so too He smites these savages for the sake of the New Covenant, so His children may enter the New Promised Land. God smites them for us. God kills them for me.

But I don't want Chickadee to die, so why would God?

I watch Chickadee's face as she falls against her father's shoulder. She pants as her nose runs. She goes limp and sleeps fitfully.

I slip on the trail and Netawatwees Sachem helps me

to my feet. "Granddaughter," he says softly, "we will stop soon."

When we rest, Chickadee drops out of her father's arms as loose and floppy as a rag doll. Her breathing sounds heavy and full of liquid. Hepte rubs her chest with an oil smelling of mint and pepper.

After supper another woman comes over to see Chickadee. She gives Hepte more oil. The oil is hot; it's been heating next to a cooking fire.

Hepte rubs the oil on her daughter's chest. Chickadee cries because the oil is hot. Other children are sick, too. We spend the night here so they can get plenty of sleep.

The overnight camp smells of mint and pepper. All the children have hot oil glistening on their chests. Even though the night is hot, they sleep shivering and whimpering next to the fire.

I lie awake and look at the stars twinkling between the darkening trees.

"God," I whisper, "I don't reckon it is Your plan, to choose me over Chickadee and the other little ones. But if it is, You don't have to choose because I don't want to be here in the first place. Send me home instead. Please."

As the wind lifts, it rustles the trees and sets the stars to hiding.

I tuck my blanket around my ankles and fall asleep before I can finish my prayers.

The mountains are gone. We are walking through high land with rolling hills.

I'm amazed that there's a trail. The trail cuts through the trees in a straight line, as though someone (something?) actually cut the trees down to make it. How can there be a trail in all this wilderness?

I ask Netawatwees Sachem that evening. "How can we be walking on a trail? There're no people here."

He smiles at me. "A long time ago, Granddaughter, the Delaware lived among animals as big as the hills. Great furry creatures with legs as big as a man and a long nose as limber as a sapling. We called them the *yah-qua-whee.*

"These animals as big as the hills liked to eat the grass. Some thought the best grass was in the east, and they would walk to the east to eat that grass. Some thought the best grass was in the west, and they would walk to the west to eat that grass.

"Animals walk in a straight line to save their strength. The animals as big as the hills made the trails by walking back and forth, east to west, west to east, unable to decide which grass was better. Their trails are still here because other animals and men continue to use them."

"These animals as big as the hills are still here?" I look around wildly.

"No. That's another story. I'll tell you sometime. Perhaps someday you will understand our stories in our language."

"I don't understand what these animals looked like."

Netawatwees Sachem draws a picture in the dirt. The animals as big as the hills look like great woolly elephants with tusks that cross in the middle.

Elephants in Ohio?

He draws a picture of spear-holding hunters surrounding the elephants. The smallest elephant's tusks are bigger than the biggest man.

"These men"–I point to the spear throwers–"are Delaware? But you used to live in the east, not here."

"That, too, is another story, Granddaughter."

I think: What wonderful farmland this ground could be. The rolling hills would be perfect protection from the wind. The soil is black, it's so rich. It's moist yet spongy, like a just-baked molasses cake. Vegetables would never rot here if it rained too much. My father would want a farm in this country–"Good drainage," he would say. Corn, pumpkins, beans, and squash could grow here as big as the hills.

After supper a few evenings later, when we are all sitting around our cooking fire, Hepte and White Eyes commence to argue. They point at me and quarrel back and forth. Hepte's eyes glow like embers as her voice becomes angrier and angrier. Chickadee's eyes fill with tears as she looks from her parents to me. Netawatwees Sachem watches me sadly.

Terror seizes me like a wolf's jaws around my throat.

"Please don't kill me–I want to live," I say. My voice comes out in a mousy squeak. "I haven't complained, not once. I haven't sp-spilled cornmeal, not a speck. Please."

My blood roars in my ears as Hepte reaches into her

knapsack. A tomahawk? A scalping knife? I open my mouth to scream.

She pulls out a pair of beaded moccasins.

Netawatwees Sachem says, "A gift, Granddaughter."

Hepte sits next to me and places the moccasins in my hands. They are the same pale yellow as butter and just as soft; the tops are covered with intricate rows of triangles and half-moon crescents. The beads glow in every shade of blue.

"They're beautiful," I say to Hepte. "Thank you."

I pull off my boots and slip on the moccasins. They fit perfectly.

"Blue is my favorite color, Grandfather. Tell her that."

After he translates, Hepte holds my face in her hands and speaks to me. She's smiling but her eyes are sad.

"My daughter says," Netawatwees Sachem translates, "the beads are like your eyes, and you must wear the moccasins only for special occasions."

"Of course," I say. "Thank you." I wriggle my toes. The beads flicker and dance like sunlight on the clearest water.

But what special occasions could these people possibly have? All eyes watch the moccasins as I pull them off regretfully and tuck them into my backpack. As I flip the cover over the top, a bit of light goes out in all their faces. Tears slip down Hepte's cheeks as she turns away.

A quiet sadness hovers around us, as though a grieving angel has gathered us in her wings. All at once I know: Hepte made these moccasins, and they once belonged to her dead daughter.

Why don't they say so?

The next morning there's a light dusting of frost on the grass!

Of course the boys try to push one another into the frost. I scrub my hands with it and pretend it's soap.

Layers of mosquito grease have worked their way into my eyes and into the corners of my mouth. The grease makes my eyes sting even worse than sweat and makes my mouth taste oily and bitter. My fingernails are black and my hands smell, they're so dirty. I can see the grime encrusted into the wrinkles of my knuckles and ankles. Will I ever be clean again?

All I think about is how tired and dirty I am and how everything hurts. Chickadee is much better and chatters away at my heels. She gives me a headache with all her talking.

The carry pack is heavy, and the cornmeal shifts with every step. At first I thought we'd be eating this corn. As the weather cools, Hepte has been giving her family the deerskin clothes from my backpack. Little by little my burden lessens. At night I dream of carrying nothing by the end of the march. But we have not touched this food.

My knees bump into the carry pack all day; they are bright red and sore by evening. My neck is bleeding by noon because the rawhide strap rubs against my skin. I learn to tuck leaves between me and the strap, and that does help a little. But my neck always feels stiff and sore.

The mornings are as chilly as the evenings now, and

the mosquitoes are gone. The mosquito grease is packed away. Thanks be to God for no more grease!

The leaves have that finished look they get right before their color turns and they begin to fall. The evening wind lifts my hair, and the sweaty skin on my forehead and neck feels cold.

One evening Hepte looks at my legs and covers her mouth with her hands. They're a mass of sores, cuts, and rashes. She says something to her father and then gives me leggings from her knapsack. They're pretty, with long fringes at the sides that swish when I walk. They have a sash at the waist and black leather straps that tie just under my knees to keep them in place. Now the underbrush and pricker bushes can't tear at my legs.

"Granddaughter," Netawatwees Sachem says, "your mother is so sorry she didn't notice your legs before now. Have courage–we will be swimming in the Cuyahoga soon."

The bodice to my birthday dress is long gone. My chemise is rent to shreds: What was once a froth of lace is now dirty cloth hanging by bits of tatting. My pretty lace collar disappeared one night. I saw it tied around a woman's wrist a few days later. My pretty lace collar from Flanders, tied around the wrist of an Indian!

The next evening Hepte digs into my backpack and gives me a long leather dress with a belt. Now I look just like everyone else except for my reddish-brown hair and blue eyes. Even my skin is as dark as everyone else's. My mother always said one can tell a lady by her milky-white skin. When will I be a lady again?

Hepte tears my chemise and fraying drawers into pieces, and every family is given strips of the cloth. I see one woman drawing a bit of lace across the back of her hand, admiring the dainty needlework. The Delaware wear lacy-white cloth bandages, slings, headbands. I even see patches of my underwear rammed down muzzles as the men load their muskets.

Now I have nothing to remind me of home. I'm wearing an old pair of moccasins, leggings, a leather dress. My hair's in braids. Even my underwear is gone. Not wearing underwear is wondrously breezy, but makes me feel even farther away from home than the wilderness does.

Wait! My grandmother Campbell's bowl from Scotland, the one with the roses painted in the bottom. What happened to it? When we stop to eat, I look intently at all the families. I don't see the bowl. A woman has hidden it away, afraid it would break on the trail or I would demand it back.

I watch the woman with my lace collar around her wrist. I'm sure she has my bowl. But her family dip their hands into a big wooden bowl filled with blackberries just like everyone else. She catches me staring at her and looks right back at me, bold as brass. It becomes a contest, who will look away first.

I look away first.

Whenever we stop to eat, Chickadee sits next to me. She chatters in my ear and gives me food from her bowl. I pretend to eat it. When I smack my lips and rub my stomach, she laughs and claps her hands. When she isn't looking, I give her food back to her. Hepte catches my eye and smiles at me.

We lie down for another night. I remember my Connecticut bed. The goose-down mattress made a great *whooshing* sound when I threw myself across it. It smelled like a henhouse–warm and cozy. I used to fluff my pillow just so before sinking my head into it. My red-and-white quilt always made me think of Christmas, even in July.

I lie awake and gaze at the stars. They look like bits of ice scattered across a parson's black cloak. The night air is downright cold. The summer's over, I think with a sinking heart. One season ending and a new one beginning and I'm walking farther and farther away.

Each evening, Mrs. Stewart finds me and lies down next to me. We whisper to each other about simple things–candle molds and rocking chairs, apple butter and hymnbooks. She tells me about growing up in Camden, New Jersey. I tell her about Fairfield, Connecticut.

"I so much want to go home," I whisper to her. "Connecticut, Pennsylvania, either will do."

"Of course you do, Mary. Say your prayers and go to sleep."

Chickadee has stopped coughing and is sleeping soundly for the first time in many a night. Her breathing sounds dry and clear. All the other children sound better, too.

Does that mean God listened to my prayer? That I'll go home someday? I watch the stars and wait for an answer.

When no answer comes, I scold my family:

Dougal, if you want to be a Mississippi trapper, you'd better learn French and how to add figures together, or the Frenchies will cheat you blind when you bring your furs into their trading posts. Try harder with the reading, Dougal. There's more to trapping than just westering farther and farther from home. You're not the stupidest boy who ever lived, but you just might be the laziest.

Pa, how could you forget my birthday? You'd better have come home that evening, proudly showing off the venison haunches that were to be my birthday dinner.

Ma, you never saw the strawberries. But I know you saw me carrying the pretty rose bowl. You must have known that I was going to pick berries for you. Why are you always so angry with me? Why is nothing I do ever good enough?

She doesn't answer.

I gaze at the stars again. It's a comfort to know we are all looking at the same stars and moon by night, the same sun by day. We even see the same clouds blowing east, although I see them first.

6

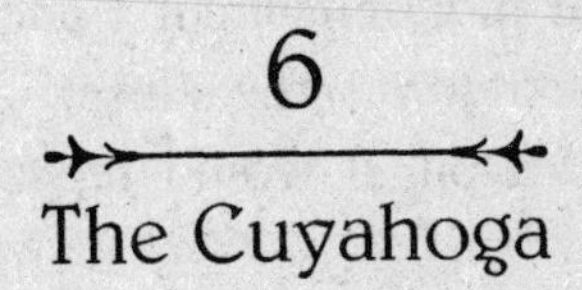

The Cuyahoga

A FEW WEEKS LATER, I reckon, we're there.

Two hundred people are standing on a cliff. Far below us a river twists and turns between the trees. There are glints and glimmers of slanting autumn sunshine against the water. A waterfall roars in the distance.

Netawatwees Sachem and some of the other men go below to look at the river. The rest of us stay huddled together. The men who remain examine the trees above us, the gorge below.

They make me nervous. Why are they so wary?

When Netawatwees Sachem and the others come back, he is holding a map, of all things, and pointing to places on it. They talk excitedly together.

I ease my carry pack to the ground. To our left drifting mist floats upward from the waterfall spray. A rainbow hangs above it. The mist feels cold against my hot face.

How good it would feel, swimming in that cold water.

The map reminds me of Dougal and his excitement about westering. It reminds me, too, of my father, always talking about the west as a golden place because it's so big and vast and empty. "Where a man has room to breathe," he'd say, pounding his chest as though there wasn't enough air in Connecticut. "The frontier–where a man's soul can stretch to the sunset."

"The frontier," Dougal would repeat with his eyes shining.

I stamp my foot and scold the Campbells again:

Silent Trapper, here's a western river, never been used. Help yourself. I'll wager you were still abed when they set fire to our cabin. And when Pa demanded to know how you could let such a thing happen, you made up a grand and glorious tale about shooting Indians through the windows and running through the forest to rescue me. Hah!

Pa, I'll bet you're sorry now. You must look at our burned-out cabin and my empty seat at the table and just feel wretched. Good. It's your fault I'm in the Ohio wilderness. And guess what–there's no more air here than in Pennyslvania or Connecticut.

Grandpa, it's your *fault I'm here. You broke Grandmother's heart tearing her away from her home. You should never have left Scotland in the first place.*

And Ma, why can't you ever–

"Granddaughter."

Netawatwees Sachem brings me back to the cliffside with a jolt. I blink at him, the Campbells floating away like dandelion cotton. Everyone else steps back to make room for me.

"I think we're here," he says pointing to the map. "Is this your thinking too?"

His map looks like Dougal's map. It has the same black lines that mean rivers and the same short, thick lines that mean words alongside the rivers. He points to the words.

He can read! Netawatwees Sachem can read a map as well as (maybe even better than) Dougal can!

I study the map. Netawatwees Sachem points to a place where the river takes a sharp turn south. He looks at me questioningly.

"Yes," I lie. But I stare at the map and don't look at him.

"Good, the Cuyahoga. I was right."

He rolls the parchment carefully. We all pick up our gear and trudge down the cliff trail to look at the winding river. The men and boys surround us; they look up at the trees as we walk.

Are they afraid of wild animals? I wonder. Other Indians?

The Cuyahoga is deep and swift, with water so clear I can see all the way to the bottom. Schools of fish push against the current. Freshwater crabs scuttle along the bottom, picking their way among smooth gray rocks.

The children want to swim, but the women shake their heads no. Now all the men are watching the surrounding cliffs. There is fear in their eyes. White Eyes climbs back up the trail with his musket cocked and ready.

"Grandfather," I whisper, "why is everyone so skittish?"

"Skittish? I don't know this word."

"Afraid."

"Ah. These are Iroquois hunting grounds, Granddaughter. We Delaware are Algonquin. The Algonquin and the Iroquois have been enemies since the *yah-qua-whee* were here. If the Iroquois are in the Oyo Hoking, we must be careful."

"But why would the British send you here if it wasn't safe? They must have told the Iroquois to stay away."

"We must hope they said nothing to the Iroquois about us coming, or they will be waiting to attack us."

It's a warm day, maybe the last warm day this year. Two hundred tired and footsore people look longingly into the river. Some reach into the current and drink from their cupped palms. Old men and women sit quietly on the riverbank and dangle their feet. The small children are jumping up and down and looking at their mothers. Their chubby arms reach toward the water.

The king's officers don't care what happens to these people, I think with a shock. If the Iroquois attack, it means two hundred fewer Indians to worry about.

The British would never have sent them here if they knew Mrs. Stewart and I were with them.

White Eyes comes back to the group and talks to the women and children. I'm surprised that I understand some of what he says. I wait for him to finish speaking.

"A good place?" I ask him in his language.

He looks at me proudly, then answers in English.

"Yes, high up on the cliff there's a cave. We'll live there through the winter and build wigwams in the spring."

We trudge up the steep cliff again. I see the cave and count how many steps I have to take to its mouth. Ten steps, nine, eight, seven, six, only five more steps, four, three, two, one. The march is over and I'm alive!

I slide the rawhide strap over my head and drop the carry pack to the ground with a thud. Freedom! I walk back and forth, enjoying the weight off my neck and shoulders. I feel lighter than air.

The cave is wide and shallow; the mouth must be a hundred feet wide, but the space is only thirty feet deep in the middle. It will keep the rain out if it's not too windy, but not much else.

Families choose their places in the cave. The women light fires, lay out animal-skin blankets, and set the baskets and bags on the cave floor. The dogs curl into a heap and lick their paws.

Incredibly, we have eaten none of the food we brought with us. Women have foraged, picking nuts, berries, and edible plants along the way. With bows and arrows men have shot rabbits and squirrels as rare treats for evening meals.

The children jump up and down and pull at their mothers' sleeves. Everyone is hot and dirty; everyone wants to swim.

"*Heh-heh,*" Netawatwees Sachem says, which is their word for "yes." With whoops and hollers, children peel off their clothes and run down the cliff trail toward the Cuyahoga.

"Tonn." Hepte has been calling me *tonn,* their word for "daughter." I turn around at her voice.

Hepte is standing in front of me with her arms outstretched and wearing nothing but a smile. Goggle-eyed, I watch grown men take off their breechcloths and leggings, their shirts and moccasins. Old women are struggling with their dresses, trying to pull them over their heads. Pregnant women are laughing and helping each other down the slope.

"K-ku," I stammer and I shake my head. *"Ku."* That means "no."

With a shrug of her shoulders Hepte runs ahead to join her family. Two hundred naked people, and they are no more aware of their nakedness than a baby would be.

Mrs. Stewart and I are the only ones left in the cave.

"Mary," she says. "We may bathe in private, when everyone else has finished. Untie this backpack for me, please."

A swim would feel so good. With sand and pebbles I could scrub the grease and campfire soot out of my skin. I could soak my hair, now stiff as a board with dried sweat, dirt, and mosquito grease, in sparkling clean, fresh water.

Far below the cliff Chickadee is laughing in the water. She's splashing one of the boys. I take everything off quickly–

"Mary!"

–and run down the cliff trail. Leafy branches brush against me as I run down toward the river.

"Mary!" Mrs. Stewart calls from the cave. "My backpack!"

My stomach is as white as the frost we left behind in the Allegheny passes. The breeze tickles in places I'd rather not consider.

The water is stirred up by the time I jump in. The river looks like the ones back in Pennsylvania and Connecticut–it looks as if people live next to it. That freshness is spoiled.

As I splash in the cool water, I try to decide if spoiling a new river is a good thing or a bad thing. Everyone is laughing and splashing everyone else. The ducks are circling above us, quacking their complaints. Box turtles have crawled out onto fallen logs to glare at us with ancient eyes.

Surely if the river is good enough for ducks and turtles, it's good enough for people, isn't it?

What's the use of a pretty, clean river if there's no one to admire its beauty? I try to imagine what the river must be thinking, if this really is the very first time people have ever gone swimming in it.

After a long swim I trudge up the cliff trail with everyone else. The small children giggle and point at my white stomach and backside. Their parents smile at them, happy to see their children laughing.

I run to untie Mrs. Stewart's backpack, but Netawatwees Sachem takes my arm and draws me to him.

"But Grandfather–"

"Don't talk to her again."

"But–"

"Not again," he says sternly. "She's nothing to you."

"But she's–"

"Tonn," Hepte says quickly. She presses a cooking pot into my hands.

Netawatwees Sachem says, "Run down the cliff trail for water. To mix with our cornmeal. Hurry, Granddaughter."

I reach for my dress and hurry down the cliff trail. I find a place upriver where the water is as clean as on the first day of Creation. I fill our cooking pot.

As the day ends, we sit on the lip of the cave, dangling our feet against the sheer rock wall.

Since we left the Allegheny, a girl about my age has tried to make friends with me. Time and again I've awakened at dawn to a little present by my shoulder–a pretty rock, a redbird feather, a lump of maple sugar. She keeps looking at me, but I won't meet her eyes. I haven't had a friend since Constance, and I don't want to disturb that memory, or Fairfield's.

Now this girl sits next to me and talks and talks–fast, as though I'm supposed to understand her.

"I don't know what you're saying," I tell her. "I don't even know your name. I can't be your friend."

"Her name is Kolachuisen," Grandfather says.

"Kola chewy sen," I repeat as the girl laughs and claps her hands. "What does her name mean, Grandfather?"

"Beautiful Bluebird."

"A bluebird!"

I clamp my hands over my eyes. I'd seen a bluebird the day before Sammy was killed. His feathers were the same color as my eyes and my birthday dress, and I'd made myself a foolish promise: I will see the Campbells again someday.

I can't bear to look at Kolachuisen. The tattered promise hurts too much.

When I finally peel my hands away from my eyes, she's gone.

The sunset turns the Cuyahoga to a ribbon of gold. We all sit and watch the sun go down. Even Mrs. Stewart is sitting with the group. Someone has untied her backpack for her.

The water shines so prettily that for the first time in a long time, I feel . . . not happy, exactly, but grateful to live, to be alive and to enjoy this sunset. It feels good to have a home again, even if it's just a cave.

The sun goes down and we go into our new home.

After our supper we sit in front of our family fires. We are all clean, cool, and well fed. Everyone is pointing at the flames and at me. Hepte has given me a comb, and I am trying to comb the tangles out of my hair.

"Granddaughter," Netawatwees Sachem says, "they are saying how fortunate we are to have someone with hair as red as the flames living among us. When it is cold this winter, they will look at your hair and feel warmer."

I look into our family fire and remember. Our hearth in Fairfield was huge, with separate compartments for roasting meats, baking breads, and simmering stews. We each had our own hearth chair. Mine was just a bench until my ninth birthday, when Pa presented me with my very own rocking chair that he had made.

"You'll rock your own babes to sleep in that chair, soon enough, Mary," he said. "Solid oak, made to last."

"Thank you, Pa. Thank you," I said to him.

Is my rocking chair just ashes now?

Chickadee crawls into my lap and puts her arms round my neck. Her hug smells faintly of mint and pepper. She has that sharp, almost sweet smell of clean water, too. I rock her in my arms, as though she's one of my own babes.

"I'm glad you're alive, Chickadee," I whisper in her ear. "God didn't choose me over you. That means my prayer was answered; I'll go home someday."

"Kamis," she shouts. *"Kamis, kamis."*

"Chickadee is saying 'sister, sister,'" Grandfather explains.

Kamis means "sister," *tonn* means "daughter." Will anyone except Mrs. Stewart ever call me Mary again?

I comb Chickadee's hair. The firelight shines darkly in her long black locks like sunlight on a raven's wings.

I braid her hair. On the other side of the family fire Hepte and White Eyes are smiling at us. Hepte gives me leather thongs for tying Chickadee's braids at the ends.

When Chickadee falls asleep in my lap, Hepte moves her to one of the blankets. Hepte sits behind me and combs my hair. It feels good, the comb dragging across my itchy scalp.

She talks softly to me. The way her voice goes up and

down, she must be telling me a story, but of course I don't understand. My eyelids start to droop. Her voice flows like the river's current, forward then stopping, forward then stopping, like water lapping against the shore.

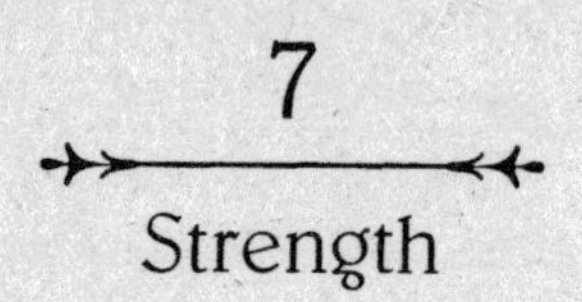

7

Strength

THE TREES FAR BELOW in the gorge slowly change color. The little round beech leaves turn to gold coins. The oaks and maples turn yellow, then orange, then red. Ash trees become as purple as plums, and the black-walnut leaves turn the same burnt-orange color as pumpkin pie.

The sparkling blue sky can only mean October.

It is beautiful . . . but Pastor Mainwood taught us that the wilderness is the Devil's domain. He said Satan is lurking, here in these forests as old as Eden, to tempt us with forbidden fruit. A city, a town, a village, a settlement, a farm, a claim–means that Satan has been driven from our midst.

He's been driven west, come to think of it.

These Delaware are as much at home in the gorge as the birds and animals. I wonder if I'll ever feel that way, no matter how long I remain in captivity. Or will I always be chary of Satan, watching out of the corner of my eye for his dark shape in the lush undergrowth?

Soon the trees' branches droop, burdened by the thousands of birds that have come to the gorge. Netawatwees Sachem says they're calling to each other by kind for the long trip south. Their calling is so loud, I can still hear them when I cover my ears. Flock by flock, great waves of birds disappear into the southern sky, taking their birdsong with them.

As the first of the winter storms blows in, the wind and rain pull all the leaves off the trees. We are left with an autumn-gold rug on the forest floor, cold wind, gray sky, bare branches, and a stark view of the river.

We awake one cold morning to snow in the gorge. The branches fill up again, with the wet snow of late autumn. The days grow colder and shorter, and the river, swollen with autumn rain and melting early snow, roars in our ears all day and all night.

Then one morning we awake to silence. The river is iced over. The long winter has begun.

We sit on stone-cold floors and lean against stone-cold walls. As our cave faces west, the westerly winds push their way inside and try to snatch the family fires away.

In Connecticut winter was always a time for fun with friends. Skating on Long Island Sound, tobogganing, rides in our neighbor's sleigh, counting redbirds, making twelve snow Apostles in the front yard every December; then long walks next to the hedgerows between the fields. Afterward we'd sit in front of a cheery fire to pop corn and drink hot apple cider. The snow-laden wind would howl outside and set the windowpanes to rattling, but snug inside our house I'd feel safe and warm.

In the cave, though, winter is something to survive. Just to get through the day is an accomplishment. The Delaware sit it out and wait patiently for spring. We sit in darkness, huddled in animal skins with only our feet and shins warmed by the fire. Like bears, everyone tries to sleep to make the time go by.

We eat pemmican–a greasy paste made from bits of meat, dried berries, and animal fat. It tastes awful and makes my tongue stick to the roof of my mouth.

Finally we're eating the food we brought from the village on the Allegheny. We dip corn meal out of my carry pack and mix it with the water from melting icicles. Hepte fries it on hot stones rubbed with deer fat.

As the snow deepens, we build a snow wall across the mouth of the cave. The wall does a fair job of keeping the wind out.

Each afternoon the women and girls leave the cave to gather firewood. Sometimes White Eyes lends me his axe. I learn to chop fallen trees into usable logs.

As kindling becomes scarce, we have to walk farther and farther from the cave to find it.

As cold as it is in the cave, it's even colder outside looking for wood. The frigid wind blows down the gorge all day and all night. We scurry back at dusk with stacks of kindling strapped to our backs and fallen branches in our arms.

At night all two hundred of us sit around the fires, our steamy breath mingling with the rising smoke. The cave walls and ceiling have turned smudgy black. When someone tells a story, he or she draws pictures on the wall by scraping away the soot with a stick. The pictures help me understand the words.

One night when Netawatwees Sachem and I are the only ones awake, I ask him to tell the story about the animals as big as the hills. I draw a picture of an elephant on the wall. "You said you had a story, Grandfather," I remind him.

"Yes, the story about the *yah-qua-whee*," he says, pointing to my drawing of the elephant.

"The *yah*-who? That's an elephant."

His eyes widen in surprise. "You have a word for this animal?"

"Elephants. They live in Africa."

"They're still alive?" he exclaims. "You've seen one?"

"I've never seen one. They're alive, though."

He leans forward. "Their fur is as thick as a bear's, and each hair is as long as a child's arm?"

"No, no fur. Africa's hot. It's across the ocean. Their skin is wrinkled and gray." Sort of like your skin, I want to say, but of course I don't.

"This changes the story," he says softly. His eyes are still wide in surprise. "This changes everything."

"Tell me the story, Grandfather."

"A long time ago, when the Creator, Kishelemukong, still walked in our gardens to admire the corn–"

"Kettle who?"

"Kishelemukong. He created us with his thoughts."

Now it's my turn to be surprised. "God?"

"As I was saying, when Kishelemukong walked in our gardens, there were the *yah-qua-whee.* The four elements–the earth, the plants, the animals, and the People–have all lived in careful balance with each other since the first days.

"But the *yah-qua-whee* did not live in careful balance with the People. They were huge and traveled in vast herds like the birds. We could hear those herds from far away, like distant thunder. They trampled our fields and crushed our corn. They roared through our villages, killing many of the People and destroying our dwellings.

"Life was harder then because it was so much colder than now. From our villages we could see ice fields as wide as the Sun's Salt Sea and as tall as mountains. It was always winter. This is why the *yah-qua-whee* needed their thick fur.

"The *yah-qua-whee* did not live in careful balance with their animal neighbors, either. They crushed burrows with sleeping animals inside and knocked over trees filled with bird nests.

"For our benefit and for the benefit of the animals, the People decided to kill all the *yah-qua-whee.* We dug huge pitfalls in the earth and hid the deep holes by weaving branches into a false floor and scattering leaves on top. Brandishing fire sticks, the People drove the *yah-qua-whee* into the deep pits. As the screaming *yah-qua-whee* were crushed against each other, their blood and flesh became soil as the pitfalls leveled out.

"When there were no *yah-qua-whee* left, the People remembered how much we needed them. One animal as big as the hills could feed an entire village for the winter. Their hides were tough enough for tents, their fur soft enough for blankets. Their great tusks were good for jewelry, and their bones were good for making tools to dig in the earth and plant our gardens.

"The People were sad. We had total victory over an enemy, but we needed that enemy. Kishelemukong was also sad, because the People had made a decision only Kishelemukong should make. He stopped walking in our gardens from that time on. No one has heard or seen Kishelemukong since.

"Maybe the animals were also sad. Who would knock the logs aside so the birds and bears could eat the insects hiding under them? Who else but the *yah-qua-whee* were strong enough, and big enough, to make the eastbound and westbound forest trails for all the animals to share? Who else would dig up the earth with their tusks while looking for roots, so the seeds could grow in the softened earth?

"That summer, as a sign to show us that we were forgiven, Kishelemukong caused the cranberries to grow from the *yah-qua-whee* pitfalls. Cranberries are as red as blood to remind us of the slaughtered *yah-qua-whee*. Like the *yah-qua-whee* the berries are good for many things: for medicine, for food, for dyes.

"The cranberries remind us that there is no such thing as total victory, and that we are not Kishelemukong. The *yah-qua-whee*, like everything else, deserved to live."

"But the elephants, Grandfather."

"Yes." He leans forward. "There are people in this Africa? And animals?"

"A lot of people and a lot of animals."

"But they didn't kill the *yah-qua-whee.* Tell me, are there cranberries in Africa?"

He holds his breath, waiting for my answer.

"I don't think so."

Netawatwees Sachem claps his hands and laughs like a child. "Then they live. The *yah-qua-whee* live!"

"How did you learn to speak English so well, Grandfather?"

He waves his hand impatiently. "That's another story. Go to sleep," he orders. "I must think about these *yah-qua-whee* of Africa. They live," he mutters to himself. "This changes everything."

There are five eight-year-old boys among us. Every morning the boys walk naked down the steep cliff trail to the river. I see their long black hair lifting and flying backward in the wind. The fathers go with them. The rest of us stand on the edge of the cliff shouting encouragement.

The fathers chop holes in the ice for the boys to jump into. The boys stay in the river for just a few moments before crawling out. When we count five boys and five fathers walking back to the cave, we all wave and cheer.

I notice the boys' mothers look anxious until their sons are safe in the cave again.

The boys' lips are blue with cold and their teeth chatter away like scolding squirrels. Their long hair freezes on the cliff trail, as stiff as tree bark. They huddle by their family fires, shivering and speaking to no one, their mothers plying them with hot tea and extra blankets.

By the afternoon the boys are finally warm.

The next morning they jump into the frozen Cuyahoga and are cold all over again.

One morning when it's sleeting and a fierce north wind blows so hard my nose aches, I ask Hepte why.

"Keko windji?" I ask. Why?

"Chitanisinen," she replies.

"Strength," Grandfather translates.

The wind howls like a wolf pack chasing down the boys' voices. Their piteous cries float upward. *"Ku, ku,"* they cry.

"Keko windji?" I ask, louder.

She looks surprised. *"Chitanisinen."*

I see these boys changing, right in front of my eyes. On the first morning they were typical eight-year-olds, throwing snowballs at each other all the way to the riverbank. As they returned, they cried for their mothers. On the second morning their fathers had switches in their hands. They beat the boys across the backs of their legs to make them walk down the cliff trail.

It's been at least four or five weeks, I think, since their first jump. Now their fathers don't need the switches. And when they return, the boys clamp their jaws shut to keep their teeth from chattering and accept blankets around their shoulders just to be polite. Two of them don't even sit by their family fires anymore. They stand outside the cave and stare at the river, the ends of their blue-black hair weighed down with milky-white ice.

Their eyes have a hardness to them, a sort of cold stare that makes it impossible to know what they're thinking.

"How long must they jump?" I ask Grandfather.

"The four winter moons–the Moon of Fallen Leaves, the Freezing Moon, the Moon of Deep Cold, and the Moon of Deep Snow. They are halfway through."

It must be close to Christmas, I think.

One day Mrs. Stewart presses a little deerskin doll into my hand. "I've lost track of the days, but merry Christmas, Mary," she whispers in my ear.

"Oh, Mrs. Stewart! I don't have anything for you."

"Just seeing your smiling face is present enough, Mary."

The doll is wearing a long dress, an apron, and a little sunbonnet on her head. I recognize the cloth–it's scraps from my birthday dress.

"My birthday dress! How? Where?"

"You left it on the trail across from Fort Pitt. Do you remember? You stepped right out of your dress when it tore away, and I knew then that you'd lost all hope."

She presses the doll harder into my palm. "This little doll is you. Always remember who you are, Mary. All my life I've heard stories about captives. The adults don't change, but the children do. They forget who they are; they forget what's important. This little doll," she repeats slowly, "is you."

I thank her and hug the doll to my chest. I don't tell her that I'm too old for dolls.

I lie awake at night thinking about the boys jumping into the frozen river every morning. Somehow they remind me of Dougal. Would he jump into icy-cold water every morning? Would his eyes have that same hard, inward look that these boys' eyes now have?

Yes, he would gladly do the same thing, to show the world how brave and strong he is.

And what about me? Don't I need strength, too?

The little doll lies next to me. When her faded blue dress reflects the firelight, she glows like a little ghost. She does make me feel stronger, but the strength she gives me is of a different kind than the strength these boys are gaining, I reckon.

These boys are learning to be Delaware braves; their newfound strength is about the future. My doll gives me the strength to remember my past.

I study my doll at night, and entire days spent in Connecticut and Pennsylvania flood into my memory. I remember what we talked about at breakfast, dinner, and supper. I remember what we ate, too: oatmeal with thick cream in the morning; ham, corn bread, pea soup, and apple slump at noon; turkey, yams, cranberries, and berry cobblers at sunset. We had bread, butter, and honey with every meal. And lots of cold milk or cider to wash everything down.

Just the thought of my mother's cooking makes my mouth water and my stomach growl.

I remember giggling with Constance Farnsworth about the silliest things–like the time her elder brother sat on a gooseberry pie, or the time my grandfather sneezed so hard he blew a candle out.

We spent long afternoons sitting on a bench near the window, looking into Constance's fancy picture book of the animal kingdom. We talked about the lions, tigers, monkeys, and elephants. While looking at the pictures we practiced being ladies. We sipped lemonade out of dainty teacups held in gloved hands, and nibbled ginger cookies with our little fingers high in the air.

Always remember who you are, Mary.

But when I start remembering, I begin to cry and can't stop.

"I need strength," I whisper, sobbing to my doll. "I need more strength than you can give me." I stuff her dress into my mouth so no one can hear me weeping.

I slept away the afternoon and now I can't sleep tonight. The family fires no longer hiss and sputter with flames but glow instead as silent embers. I imagine myself strolling right into Campbell Station next spring. The dogwoods are white and yet the most delicate pink from a distance. In the pasture the tender grass smells sweet. Livestock are treading on the wild strawberries again. Spring lambs and calves cleave to their mothers.

Dougal is still sitting on his stupid rock in the middle of the pasture, mooning over his map.

"Good afternoon, Dougal," I say.

Seeing me dressed the way I am, he jumps clean into the air, thinking I'm an Indian. The map lands in the mud.

"Mary?" he says, his eyes as big as wagon wheels. "Ma! It's Mary! She's home!"

My mother, dressed in black, is sitting on the side porch dolefully churning butter. She jumps off the porch and charges toward me, skirts flying.

"Mary," she hollers out. "Mary's come home!"

My father runs toward us from the fields, holding his sun hat flat against his head so it won't blow away. Even Lady Grey is purr-winding around my ankles. My mother enfolds me in her arms.

"I'm all right. I escaped. I'm all right."

"Oh Mary! And it's your birthday, too! I'll make you a cake and everything!"

As we walk toward the cabin, I can't go another step until I've given them all a piece of my mind.

"Pa, if you hadn't made us go westering, this would never have happened. I've been starving, freezing, terrified, and so exhausted I've fallen asleep with half-chewed food in my mouth. You're so selfish. You only think about yourself."

He hangs his head. "I'm sorry, Mary. We'll go back to Connecticut tomorrow, just as you wish."

I turn to Dougal.

"And you, you were supposed to be protecting me. If you hadn't been so lazy, I might never have been kidnapped."

Dougal hangs his head. "I'm sorry, Mary. I'll never sleep beyond daybreak again. My lazy days are over."

I turn to Ma.

"And you, you were always so angry with me. Nothing I ever did was good enough. Why did you make my life so hard?"

She hangs her head and speaks so softly I have to lean forward to hear her. "Because a woman's life is hard, Mary, much harder than a man's. It breaks my heart to be the one to prepare you for your future, for all I want is your happiness."

I sit bolt upright, half expecting to see my mother kneeling between the dark lumps of sleeping Delaware. It's a long time before sleep comes.

We awake one dawn to the most direful cold–the bitterest, coldest morning I can remember.

Hepte rubs mosquito grease on our faces and hands to keep our skin from cracking. Frigid wind screams down the gorge and sets the trees to shivering. It hurts to breathe. I squirm in front of a weak and quavering fire, my teeth chattering and my bladder full.

The boys try to look brave and unconcerned, but I can see the fear in their eyes. Holding blankets and axes, the fathers go down the cliff trail with them. We hear the ice cracking as the fathers chop holes in the ice for their sons. We hear the boys scream as they climb out of the ice holes. The boys run stiff legged up the cliff trail with blankets around their shoulders.

Their fingers are blue. Their cracked heels are bloody from running on the sharp stones. Everyone is paying attention to the boys, rubbing their feet, spooning hot cornmeal into their mouths, pushing cups of hot tea into their hands.

Now, I say to myself. *I need more strength.*

I pick up the axe White Eyes lets me use for firewood. "I get wood," I say in their language, "good fires for the boys."

Hepte tries to catch my hand. "Tonn," she says softly.

I walk quickly down the cliff trail and shed my clothes on the riverbank. I walk to the center of the river. My heart is pounding as I begin chopping. It takes longer than I think it will to chop a hole in the thick ice. I toss the axe next to my clothes.

Now! I am already shivering as I jump in.

The cold shocks the air right out of my lungs. I curl into a ball, and that is my mistake. The swift current sweeps me away from my ice hole.

I can't breathe! I'm under the ice! I pound the underside of the ice with my fists. It doesn't break.

When I open my eyes in the cold, dim water, I see an ice hole from when the boys jumped in. My hands break through the thin membrane of ice already forming across it. The current pushes me forward and the ice hole slips away from my grasp.

I look forward again. There are four more ice holes, each one with a dimly lit column of water underneath. One of the columns has two arms and an angry face dangling upside down within it.

A face?

White Eyes grabs my hair as I rush by. I try to grasp his arms but my fingers don't work.

He pulls me out of the ice hole by the hair and throws me onto the snow. I fall like a sack of potatoes. The wind freezes me to the bone.

"Get up!" he roars at me in English. "Get up!"

He has a switch in his hand. I watch him switching my legs. I don't feel anything.

I try to stagger upright but my legs don't work. White Eyes hoists me to my feet and I stumble to the riverbank.

He is already there, holding the axe and my clothes.

"Run!" he screams at me. "Run!"

Gasping for breath, I stumble up the cliff trail as he chases after me. I hear the switch singing against my legs, but he might as well be hitting fence posts; I don't feel a thing.

My hair is frozen stiff. My numb and bleeding feet flip and flop like fish on the icy rocks. My teeth chatter, then my jaw clamps shut. Ice has coated my eyelashes; the ice scratches against my eyes. My fingers are bluish white by the time we reach the cave.

Hepte is waiting. She scoops me up in a blanket and holds me tightly in front of the fire. Chickadee rubs my feet.

White Eyes shouts at me, but I don't understand a thing. Mrs. Stewart shouts at me too, but I don't understand her, either. Grandfather pushes her out of the way and shouts some more. I just stare at them all–my mind is as stiff and frozen as my body. Their shouting is muffled and dim, as though coming from a great distance. My eyelids start to droop. I could sleep for days.

"No!" Grandfather shouts. He shakes me hard by the shoulders. "Mary! Mary Caroline Campbell! Don't sleep," he shouts in my ear as he pinches my cheeks. He hoists me to my feet and walks with me. We weave in and out between the family fires. We walk for a long time.

The backs of my legs begin to sting. Then my fingers, ears, and nose throb with sharp, hot pain. My thoughts come back slowly, like dying coals coaxed and stirred to fiery life.

I collapse in Hepte's arms again.

"I need more strength," I gasp to her. "I don't have enough strength."

"Shh. I will tell you a secret," Hepte murmurs in my ear. She rocks me in her lap. "Tell me when you are ready to hear this secret."

Chickadee presses my doll into my right hand. My fingers close around the doll, as slow and creaky as an old woman's fingers.

Hepte waits for me as I shiver and shiver. Finally, I nod.

"Secret," I say in a shaky voice. It occurs to me, slowly, that I spoke to her in her own language and that I can understand what she is saying to me. But Hepte doesn't speak a word of English.

She whispers in my ear, "I saw you chopping a hole

in the ice and sent your father down the cliff trail to pull you out. This is the secret: You have more strength than any of these boys. And you do not have to jump into a frozen river to prove it."

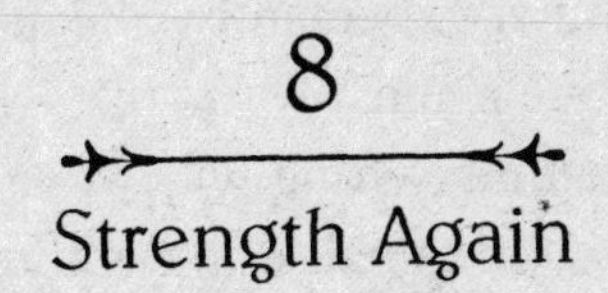

8

Strength Again

WILL THIS WINTER EVER BE OVER?

The days turn warm, and just when I think perchance it really is spring, the snow blows down the gorge again, reminding me that there's plenty of winter left.

Then the weather turns pied: wet snow; sunshine; sleet; rain mixed with snow; sunshine again; sleet again; more wet snow.

We have to go farther and farther afield to look for firewood. Mrs. Stewart always walks alone as she looks for wood. When she comes back to the cave at dusk, her eyes are red from weeping.

Now that the winter is almost over, I want to plan our escape. We could be home in time for my birthday.

But Chickadee tags after me every afternoon. Most of the wood she picks up is either too heavy for her, so I end up carrying it, or so rotten and soggy as to be useless.

Today, however, she's napping back in the cave. I follow Mrs. Stewart past the waterfall, past the bend, and all the way to where beavers have dammed up the Cuyahoga, turning it into a deep pool.

I call out, "Mrs. Stewart?" She jumps.

"You frightened me, Mary."

"Look." I give my left earlobe a tug with my right hand and look at her expectantly. She just frowns at me, so I tug my earlobe again.

"Is there something wrong with your ear, Mary?"

"That's my escape signal–don't you remember?"

"Shh." Mrs. Stewart draws me close. "I told you not to say that word." She looks around us wildly.

"No one can hear us."

"We can't leave. How could we cross the Appalachians with snow as deep as a house?"

My eyes fill with tears. "But it's almost spring."

"Not in the mountains."

"You said we could escape. You promised."

"I said I'd promise to think about it. But it's much too dangerous, Mary. We'll just have to wait for a rescue."

"Are you saying we're not going to try? All this winter I've been telling myself we'd be home by my birthday," I cry out. "How could you betray me this way?"

"I haven't betrayed you. Not another word."

"That's what my mother used to say when she'd run out of words," I say bitterly.

Mrs. Stewart is already walking ahead of me on the trail, not listening.

"You're content to die here, aren't you? Mrs. Stewart?"

I call out. "Just rot here and die? You're not even going to try?"

She gives her kindling strap a pull to hitch the firewood higher onto her back. She doesn't stop walking.

I come back at dusk with more kindling strapped to my back and fallen branches in my arms. I walk through the frozen gorge surrounded by bleak trees. This is what it feels like when all hope is lost, I think. I might as well be these barren trees, reaching up to a darkening gray sky. And waiting for a spring that will never come.

But spring always returns, no matter how raw and long the winter remains. I can't give up hope.

"Believe in the bluebird's promise, Mary," I say out loud. "Believe in yourself. I will see my family again someday."

A thin ribbon of hope glows within me, just as the Cuyahoga shines like molten iron as it reflects the setting sun.

The next morning White Eyes comes back to the cave with a doe he's killed. While I collect firewood, Hepte makes a savory stew of venison, dried squash, and powdered mushrooms.

After she sets up our fill of the meat for smoking, Hepte divides the rest among the other families. Now every family fire has a stewpot bubbling with venison and vegetables. The cave is steamy with the comforting fragrance of hot food.

This is not unusual. Other hunting parties have come

back to the cave with game. The hunters' wives cook enough for their families, then share the rest.

The next day Grandfather explains that Hepte wants my help to tan the deerskins. "You will not have to gather wood today, Granddaughter. And soon you'll have a new pair of leggings. You're growing so fast; Hepte has noticed yours are too small."

"Heh-heh," I say to Hepte, and she smiles at me.

With a great flourish of prayers and face paint, the men and boys leave for another hunting expedition. Sometimes I think hunting is just an excuse for the men to escape the cave. Most of the time they come back empty-handed. You'd think they'd look more chagrined and disappointed.

I stand on the cliff trail and watch them longingly as they march out into the fresh, cold air. A bright curtain of sunbeams breaks through the clouds, filling the gorge with pearly light. Just like home, I think with a sigh. The men and boys leave, the women and girls stay behind and do the work.

"Tonn," Hepte says, pointing to the place next to her. Just as I sit down, she flings the deerskin out onto the cave floor.

The deerskin is already stiff, the skin side scraped but still bloody with spiderwebby sinew clinging in places.

She reaches for a covered bowl and places it between us. When she takes the cover off, I feel as though someone has punched me in the stomach.

The bowl is filled with lumpy gray matter crisscrossed with blood vessels like dark lace. The doe's brains.

I gasp. For once even Chickadee is silent, staring wide-eyed.

Hepte pulls down her leggings and straddles the bowl.

After living in a cave all winter with two hundred Delaware, I think I've smelled and seen and heard just about everything people do.

But I've never seen anyone empty her bladder in the cave. We always go outside.

Hepte stands and pulls up her leggings. "Tonn," she says, pointing to the bowl.

"Keko windji?" I whisper. What can she be thinking?

She says something, and Chickadee pulls down her leggings and straddles the bowl. Chickadee smiles up at me as a little bit trickles out. She stands up, points to the bowl, and chatters at me about a mile a minute.

Gray lumps of brain float and bob in a pool of yellow urine. It looks like sour milk long gone to curd. Hepte and Chickadee look at me expectantly.

"Ku," I say, shaking my head. *"Ku,* Hepte."

Hepte shrugs her shoulders, then sets to work. She dips her hands into the steaming mess and mixes it into a paste. She begins to rub the paste into the bloody side of the deerskin. Chickadee helps, the gray mass curling out between her chubby fingers.

I can't bring myself to look for more than a moment or two. It occurs to me, as I'm looking down at my tunic, that my butter-soft leather clothes and beaded moccasins were tanned by Hepte, and surely in the same way. And that's the same bowl we've used for our family dinners. The same pot we eat from. How could she–

"Tonn," Hepte says angrily. "Tonn. *Mary*."

When I turn around she's unrolling a much smaller skin. She gives the bowl a bit of a push in my direction and points to the little pelt. There's still a bit of the brains-and-urine paste sloshing in the bowl.

I kneel down in front of the skin. At first I think it's a rabbit skin, but it has four long strips jutting out where the legs used to be.

"What is this?" I ask in Unami.

Hepte says something, but I shake my head.

"I don't understand."

She points to the deerskin with one hand and makes a rounded motion over her stomach with the other.

"The doe was pregnant?" I gasp in English. "This was . . . her fawn?"

I spring to my feet and run toward the riverbank.

"No more," I gasp. And if I could stamp my foot while running down the cliff trail, I'd do so.

I hang my head over the water. At first I think I'm going to be sick, but the fresh air and gulps of clean water clear my head and ease my stomach.

Hepte wants me to put my hands in that horror! My hands are swollen and red, the palms cracked and bleeding from cold wind and icy water. They haven't touched soap in almost a year. But they're still my hands, hands that once played Handel on the pianoforte, hands that once held dainty plates and cups for afternoon teas.

I remember the soup from last night. I'd never tasted meat so tender and soft.

That was the baby, the unborn fawn!

Now my breakfast does come up. While I'm on my hands and knees, my stomach heaves again and again, as though by vomiting long enough, and hard enough, I could rid myself of everything that has happened to me.

I curl up by a tree and sob and sob. "Why?" I wail to the four winds. "Why did this happen to me?"

Escape, Mary. Run. You've got the strength, don't you? Stop waiting for a trapper or the king's men to come and rescue you. It may be years before anyone comes this way. If ever. Mrs. Stewart hasn't the nerve to run. She'll rot here, in misery and despair, for the rest of her life.

I run south down the river trail.

"South by southeast," I say aloud as I stumble over rocks and tree roots, "and then over the mountains. I've done it once–I can do it again. I'll be home by May. I'll eat the leaves as they come out, the berries, the acorns. I'll find . . . find wild strawberries in the meadows. These Indians have been foraging for generations. I'll find enough to eat."

At this very moment Constance is wearing a pretty dress and sitting in a warm and tidy schoolhouse, learning to read. Why should I have to live like an animal? Why should I never see Constance or my family again, never eat at a table again, never sleep in a bed again? It's not my fault Hepte's daughter died. Why do I have to pay the price?

I laugh out loud. "Not westering, eastering," I shout.

The Campbells . . . I *will* see my family again by my birthday!

What if trappers never do come here? What if the king's men decide the Cuyahoga is too far away and never come here to rescue me? What will happen? I'll live here the rest of my life, that's what will happen.

Run away! Don't stop! Strength. Chita . . . nee . . . something.

I trip over a tree root and sprawl into the late-winter slop. As I get up, I look behind me: One set of telltale footprints settling into the wet snow and mud. Tracking me would be as easy as tracking a *yah-qua-whee.*

Mary Caroline Campbell, what do you reckon you're doing?

It must be three hundred miles to the Susquehanna. Three hundred miles of forests filled with hungry wolves, bears, and panthers. The Alleghenies are still covered with snow, and the passes must be freezing cold at night. For all I know, we're still at war with the French. That means they'd march me to Quebec City as a prisoner of war if they caught me.

And what would these Delaware do to you if they caught you?

You don't have a knife, Mary. Even if you knew how to load and shoot a musket, you don't have one. You don't have flint to start a fire. Your clothes are too small. You don't even have a blanket to keep out the cold.

"And what am I so all fired up about going home to?" I say bitterly. "A brother who thinks calling me a *girl* is the worst insult there is. A mother who treats her son as a prince and her daughter as a slave. A father who dragged me away from my home and my best friend without so much as a backward glance."

But don't I owe it to my parents to escape? Don't I owe my king at least an attempt to escape?

Grandfather says the name Cuyahoga means "crooked river" in Cayuga, one of the Iroquois languages. The path has zigged and zagged every which way, following the river. I can't see our cave. Even our cliff has disappeared around the bend.

There might be not another person on earth but me.

I shiver as the wind blows cold against my face and limbs. It seems to blow right through my hollowed stomach. How good it would feel to sit in front of our family fire, warm and safe.

What about yourself, Mary? What do you owe yourself?

I owe myself my life and a chance for happiness.

Go back now before they reckon you tried to escape. Do whatever you have to do in order to survive. King, country, parents, friendship–they won't mean anything if you're dead.

Back in the cave, Hepte and Chickadee are stretching the skins and hanging them over the fire. When Hepte sees my face, swollen and red from crying, she looks at me questioningly.

"Hepte," I say softly, "*kamis* Chickadee."

I begin to apologize, but Hepte puts her arms around me.

"*Ku, ku,*" she says softly. "Tonn."

She holds my face in her hands. They're wet but I tell myself not to think about why.

"Everything's so different," I cry out in Unami. "Everything's so different with you people. It's . . . so hard."

A flicker of understanding lights her eyes.

"Don't tell on me . . . please," I plead with her. "Don't tell your father I tried to leave."

"*Heh-heh. Chitanisinen, Tonn,*" she says slowly.

I nod, recognizing the word for "strength."

"*Chitanisinen lappi, Tonn,*" she says.

Strength again, Daughter.

"*Heh-heh,*" I reply. "*Chitanisinen lappi.*"

"Our secret. It took strength to leave," Hepte says slowly, "but so much more to return."

9

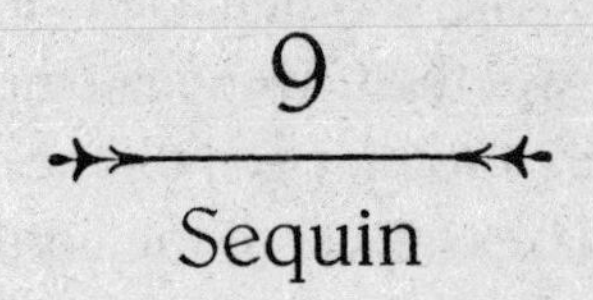

Sequin

SOMEONE FROM ANOTHER FAMILY FIRE makes up a story about the People and the winter as a great, hibernating bear. "We are in the jaws of the bear. The wind is the bear's snores, wheezing and howling through its huge teeth."

Everyone smiles and nods and points to the icicles hanging down, fanglike, from the top lip of the cave. The snow wall looks like a bear's bottom lip.

The icicle fangs grow longer and longer. The days are a little warmer now, so the ice melts as the sun shines. But the nights are still cold, so the dripping water freezes once the sun is down. One of our icicles has frozen all the way to the floor of the cave. It's one solid piece of ice.

The ice on the river snaps and breaks. The cracking ice sounds like the booming of cannon fire and makes me think of British soldiers, finally coming to rescue me.

Our snow wall begins to melt. Water trickles inward, and in some places the uneven cave floor is ankle deep with icy water. One morning we push the snow wall over the side. We all blink at one another in the bright sunlight.

I can see the river again from the cave. The swift current spins the floating ice chunks into a delicate minuet.

Grandfather says the Cuyahoga empties into a great lake, so wide the other side can't be seen. He says there are even bigger lakes farther to the north, with waves as big as ocean waves.

I didn't know we were so close to the French lakes. We're at war with France.

My heart beats a little faster and my mouth goes dry.

He says the French call this lake Lac du Chat, Cat Lake, because it was named after the Erie, the People of the Panther.

"It was the French who first traded with them, but the Erie have disappeared," he explains. "The French call the lake after the Erie to remember them."

I frown at the river. "There is something odd about the Cuyahoga," I say to him.

Grandfather nods. "It flows north. Most rivers flow south."

"Of course! How strange."

"Soon we'll go to Sequin, and you'll see why this river flows north. You can read, Granddaughter. You'll go with us and help us. Sequin will have treaties and declarations for us to look at." Grandfather sighs. "To white men, the spoken word means even less than the written."

"Who is Sequin?" I ask with a sinking heart.

You can read.

"A fur trader. His trading post is downriver and near the great Erie lake."

"Sequin," I say uneasily. "But you can read. Why must I go?"

He looks disappointed. "This is your chance to help."

"Oh." I swallow hard. "Of course, Grandfather."

On the first really warm day, Grandfather announces that it's time to go to Sequin's. Grandfather, White Eyes, and two other men watch as I pack food into my carry pack. The only food we have left is that awful greasy pemmican.

As I press the pemmican into leather pouches, I think about my mother's flapjacks–crisp around the edges and soft in the middle. Dougal and I ate them by the platterful with bacon and maple syrup, and butter if we had any. We washed the flapjacks down with new milk. If it was a special occasion, Christmas or a birthday, we sipped a delicious, smoky-tasting tea called Pekoe that came all the way from China.

The boys no longer jump into the river every morning. They do look harder, impassive. Ever since I jumped into the river, I see grudging respect for me in their eyes. Now, as we leave, I see envy in their eyes, too. They're as bored with the cave as I am and are looking for adventure. I'm too embarrassed to meet their gaze for long. Netawatwees Sachem is counting on me for help, and he's going to find out I can't help him because I can't read. They're all going to find out.

I carry the food and the men carry the furs they'll trade at Sequin's. We pick our way down the muddy cliff trail and alongside the river. We walk till noon before stopping to rest.

There are no leaves yet on the bare trees, barer still because the trunks are stripped of their bark. The deer are so hungry in early spring, they'll eat even bark to survive.

Water is flowing everywhere. It trickles from between the rocks hanging over the river. It drips down the cliff sides and lands on our heads. It gurgles down the path, filling our moccasins with cold mud. Streamlets overflow; tiny waterfalls tumble from rock to rock.

All the water flows into the swollen river. The Cuyahoga roars by in a tangle of broken branches and trees. Chunks of ice spin in the whirlpools. We make slow progress, stepping around mires and fallen logs.

We stop to rest again, to nibble on a few bites of pemmican and to wring out our moccasins. My stomach growls loud enough for everyone to hear.

"Now is the Sugar Maple Moon, but it's also known as the Starving Moon," Grandfather says. "We're grateful the winter is over, but there's still no food. Soon the Cuyahoga will give us fish big enough to catch. For now we can always eat bark."

Bark?

At dusk it begins to rain hard. The swollen river

edges closer and closer to the path. We find another cave, much smaller and deeper than ours. White Eyes steps in cautiously and comes out shaking his head. Even though I'm tired, I listen intently.

"*Makwa*," he mutters. He holds up three fingers.

"A mother and her cubs?" Grandfather asks in Unami. "Are they still sound asleep? Will we disturb them if we stay the night?"

White Eyes shifts uncomfortably on his feet. "They are sound asleep for now, Father-in-law."

"Three bears?" I ask. "In the cave?"

Grandfather nods and replies in English. "We will have a cold camp and share their cave for the night." They all look at me. "The rain comes down harder now and my granddaughter is tired."

White Eyes looks at him as though he's gone mad.

We step slowly inside. I can't see the bears, but I hear the even breathing of the mother and her cubs, still deep in hibernation. The slow, rhythmic breathing rumbling out of the mother bear's chest throbs like a great beating heart. One of the cubs has a snore like a whistle; the other sounds just like its mother only higher in pitch.

I can smell them, too. The mother has a sharp, sour smell, so that sweet-as-honey scent must come from the cubs. The bears give off heat from their corner of the cave. It's almost like having a fire.

When my eyes adjust to the gloom, I can see them, three balls of inky black against the dark cave wall.

We all lie down warily and wait for sleep to come. I unpack a blanket and pretend I'm one of the bear cubs, snug against my mother's fur. I fall asleep almost instantly.

In the morning we make haste to leave. Morning sunbeams light up the cave as the bear family slumbers on. The mother is a huge black bear, and her cubs look to be about the size of human babies.

What I see makes my hair stand on end.

"One of the cubs is nursing–it's awake!" I whisper.

"They nurse while asleep," Grandfather explains. "We haven't disturbed them."

"More importantly, Grandfather, they haven't disturbed us."

He has brought men who can speak English on this trip to Sequin's. They all laugh softly at my little joke.

The mother bear snorts and we charge out of the cave.

Later this morning I can scarcely believe my good fortune. There, resting on a tree branch as though God in all His wisdom meant for only me to find it, is a bluebird feather. It glows as blue as an October sky.

I brush the feather against my cheeks. "Thank you, thank you," I murmur. Whom do I thank? God, for allowing me to find it? The bluebird, for leaving a tail feather behind? Or myself, for having the patience and courage to believe in my own promise? A promise delayed is not a promise denied. I will go home someday.

I place the feather lovingly in my carry pack as far as possible from the greasy pemmican.

By late afternoon on the third day I see a curl of

smoke far ahead on the horizon. The Cuyahoga straightens out and widens as we walk closer to the Lac du Chat. The ice chunks are farther apart, but still spinning around and around.

Soon my nostrils fill with the musky smell of marine life–the sand, the fish, the vegetation on shore. Seagulls hang almost motionless in the sky, pushing against a brisk wind. Long-legged water birds–terns and plovers–pick their way delicately in the shallows, looking for food.

On the horizon the smoke curl becomes a chimney. A bit later the chimney becomes a rooftop and finally a cabin.

I stop and think for a moment. "Bit by bit, we've been walking downhill," I say. "All this time. Is that why the river flows north? It flows downhill toward the lake?"

Grandfather nods. "You've thought it out for yourself," he says proudly.

Sequin's cabin and trading post is on the eastern shore of the river just where it meets the lake. The cabin has a wraparound porch and sits on a beach of fine white sand.

The Lac du Chat stretches far to the north, as far as I can see. The horizon is a dark-blue smudge where the sky, low-lying clouds, and water meld together.

On summer days back home Constance and I used to wrap corn bread and apples in a clean napkin and spend the day at Pine Creek Point or Fairfield Beach. I remember gazing at the Sound, unable to understand how there could be so much water in the world.

Lac du Chat looks like the Atlantic, or at least Long Island Sound. Waves crash to the shore, as big as ocean waves. They drag the pebbles away from the beach with a grating sound as the waterbirds chase the retreating surf, looking for clams and fingerlings washed up on shore.

I taste the water. It *is* fresh, fresh and cold.

"May I stay out here, Grandfather? To look at the lake?"

"We need your help."

As we enter the cabin, my heart is pounding, and not just because I can't read. The whole cabin reminds me of home! While the men talk, my gaze darts everywhere, eager to find things I remember. Comfortable chairs are arranged around the fireplace; the fire crackles with an invitation to sit and rest a spell, warm the hands and feet. Pretty jars and brass lamps decorate the mantelpiece. A dining table and matching chairs grace the far corner. From the doorway I spy a second room with a fancy carved bed, a lace coverlet, and fluffy pillows.

Then I notice the dirt. Next to the fireplace muddy shoes give off steam and stink of feet. Dirty bowls and silverware clutter the furniture. Here and there, grimy clothes have drifted and piled like snow. Clinging to the spotty windows are cobwebs and caramel-colored spider-egg sacs. In the far corner the beautifully carved table is covered with cook pots and fly-blown crockery.

As soon as I see the dirt, I know Sequin doesn't have a wife.

On the other side of the room is his merchandise. He

must do a brisk business in trade, I reckon. I've seen the objects the Delaware treasure, and he has just the sort of brightly colored finished goods they like. Papers of needles and pins, and glass jars full of bright candy crowd the countertop. Spools of thread, bolts of colored cloth, copper kettles, jewelry, brushes and combs, jugs of rum–anything the Indians might want.

I pounce on a little paper-covered packet sitting on a shelf. I bring it to my nose and take a deep sniff. Soap! Soap that smells like roses! I sniff and sniff until I can't smell it anymore.

Sequin's thick dark hair and beard remind me of the black bears in the cave. Standing behind the counter, he stares at me in surprise as I smell the soap, then motions me to come forward. As I walk toward the counter, he reaches into a drawer and pulls out a piece of paper.

First he bows. "François Sequin, mademoiselle," he says.

My first impulse is to curtsy, but I stop myself. What would my parents think of me, showing respect to a dirty Frenchy! A people we've been at war with for going on seven years!

"Mary Caroline Campbell," I say stiffly.

"Come! You tell men!" he shouts at me.

I glance at Grandfather, who nods to me and smiles. *What will he do when he finds out I've lied to him about reading?* I think in panic. *Maybe I'll tell him I've forgotten how.*

Sequin hands me an official-looking document. The red wax seal is broken; the ink on the paper is in great flourishes and curlicues. There are drawings of lions and fleurs-de-lis in the four corners.

The squiggly lines mean absolutely nothing. My hands are shaking and my mouth is dry. "I can't read this," I whisper to Grandfather. "I'm sorry."

He looks shocked; then his eyes blaze in anger.

Sequin snatches the paper from my hands.

"*Tu parles français?*" he shouts at me. "Speak French, little one?"

He turns into a watery blur as I shake my head.

Sequin stabs the paper with a grimy finger.

"Netawatwees Sachem. French king say welcome," he shouts. "Ohio French land. French king. French Sequin. Trade here only."

"Of course!" Relief floods over me. "This writing is in French, Grandfather. I–I can't read French."

"It say . . ." Sequin points to the document. "Welcome to king's land. Welcome. Trade with Sequin only. French king. French Ohio. French goods. French Sequin."

"This isn't French land," I retort. "My father says this land belongs to us. This is the Western Reserve. It was reserved by King Charles II almost one hundred years ago. This is British land."

Sequin looks enraged. "*Non!* French land! French king! French Sequin! France! France! France!" he shouts. Every time he shouts "France!" Sequin pounds the countertop so hard, he makes the bar of soap and glass candy jars jump.

"Yes," Grandfather says softly. "We trade only with you." He points to the lake outside. "French lake, too."

"*Oui*." Sequin's mouth stretches into a toothless smile. "Lac du Chat. French land. French king. French goods. French Sequin."

The men put their peltry on the counter. They trade them for cloth, kettles, gunpowder, and shot. White Eyes points to a jug of rum on a top shelf, but Grandfather snarls at him before Sequin can reach for it. White Eyes looks sheepish and shakes his head. Sequin just shrugs his shoulders.

Sequin reaches into a glass candy jar and hands me a bright-red cinnamon stick. When he smiles at me, I notice he has dried tobacco juice in the creases of his lips and bits of moldy food in his beard. He smells just like that mother bear back in the cave.

"Thank you, sir." I take the cinnamon stick quickly. Despite my haste, he's left grimy fingerprints all over it.

"*Merci*," Grandfather says. "*Au revoir, Monsieur Sequin*." He turns to leave.

"You speak French?" I shout in amazement, tagging at his heels. "French *and* English?"

"*Attendez, Sachem des Indiens*," Sequin calls out. "*Attendez, s'il vous plaît*."

We turn around. Sequin starts at my toes and, taking his time, allows his eyes to linger here and there as he looks at me all the way up to my hair. As he licks his slobbery grin, I step backward and backward again.

Sequin places three shiny new muskets on the counter. "*Belle jeune fille*," he says, nodding at me. He pats the muskets with one hand and points toward me with the other.

"*Non,*" Grandfather says. "She's my granddaughter. *Elle est ma petite-fille, Monsieur Sequin.*"

Sequin puts another musket on the counter and looks at him expectantly.

"*Non, monsieur,*" Grandfather says politely. "My granddaughter, *ma petite-fille.*"

Sequin points to the rum and looks at White Eyes.

"*Non,*" Grandfather says quickly. "*Au revoir, monsieur.*"

Sequin shrugs his shoulders and puts the muskets back on the shelf behind him.

"*C'est dommage, mais c'est la vie.* This is life, no? *Bon voyage, Netawatwees, Sachem des Indiens.*"

As he grins at me, his eyes glow. "Mademoiselle Marie, I will see you again very soon."

That night at our campfire Grandfather stares at the fire for a long time, lost in his own thoughts.

"Granddaughter," he says finally, "are there many French people? More than the Iroquois but less than the English?"

"I don't know. More than the Iroquois. Probably the same as the English."

"All those French," Grandfather says with a grin, "and lucky for us only one Sequin."

I laugh. My secret is safe.

"We must keep Sequin happy so he will not raise his prices," he says softly. "We must all do what we can."

My heart starts pounding. "Don't send me back there. I'll work harder. I'll learn your language. Please."

He looks shocked. "Do you think I'd let my granddaughter marry a dirty Frenchman?"

I don't know what to think, except to change the subject.

"Um . . . What happened to the Erie? I never see anyone on the river but ourselves."

"One hundred years ago, the Iroquois wanted the Oyo Hoking to be their hunting grounds. The Erie were in the way, so they were all killed by the Iroquois."

"Who does Sequin trade with if nobody lives here?"

Grandfather looks at me strangely. "There are many nations in the Oyo: The Wyandot to the west, the Miami to the south, the Shawnee who live along the Muskingum River."

"Would the Iroquois really kill us if they thought we were in the way, too?"

"We have treaties with them, but they are Iroquois. And we've been enemies forever. You can't read," he says softly.

My blood jumps. "I can't read French–"

"No." His rough hand closes around my wrist like a snare.

"Never lie to me again," he says softly. But I can hear the anger in his mild voice, like embers glowing beneath a dying fire.

"I'm sorry."

"You people only know how to lie. You don't know how to speak the truth." He squeezes my wrist tighter.

"I speak the truth."

"No," he says, squeezing harder.

"You know how to speak English and French," I stammer. My hand begins to throb. "You know about the Cuyahoga flowing north and what happened to the Erie. You know about the grasslands to the west and what happened to the *yah-qua-whee.* I'm ashamed to be ignorant and I'm angry because it's not my fault. Men want girls to be pretty and sweet and stupid. That's the truth."

"I see." He lets go of my wrist. In the firelight I see white marks where his fingers were.

After a bit I say, "You went to school, Grandfather?"

"When I was eight years old, I, too, jumped into a frozen river every morning during the four winter moons. I jumped into the Susquehanna." He stares intently at the fire. "My village was close to your Campbells' cabin."

"It–it was?" I stammer.

"Afterward, I went to a boys' school in Philadelphia. I studied English, French, Latin, mathematics, and European history. I haven't read English or French for years, and an old man forgets. We studied geography, but we didn't study your Africa. I would have liked knowing about the elephants before now."

I stare at him with my mouth open. Will this man ever stop surprising me?

"Why . . . why did you go to school?"

"I was to be the leader of the Delaware someday. I had to learn so many things."

"You can read a map?"

"Of course. The British gave me that map. What

would they think of me if they thought I couldn't read one of their maps?"

"The same way you think about me," I say softly. My chin quivers, my mouth crumples. Hot tears slide down my cheeks.

He doesn't say anything for a long time. Then: "Never call me 'grandfather' again."

"I'm sorry," I cry, sobbing harder.

"You misunderstand me," he says gently. "Call me *muxomsa*. It means 'grandfather.' Try it."

I sniff and wipe my eyes with the backs of my arms.

I try it. "Moo CHUM sa." It sounds like a sneeze.

"Granddaughter is *nuxkwis*. *Nuxkwis*, you don't know how to read, but you're learning our language well. From this time forward, no English."

"Yes. I mean, *heh-heh, Muxomsa*. But . . . what about talking to Mrs. Stewart? She doesn't speak your language."

"No English. Mrs. Stewart was a mistake," he says flatly. "She is an angry, bitter woman who likes to eat but doesn't like to work. I gave her as a second wife to Tamaqua, but he tells me she's a hateful wife."

"That's not hate, it's grief. It was you who gave the order for Sammy to be killed."

"Who?"

"Her baby!"

"Her baby," he repeats softly. "Yes, I remember Sammy. We had to hurry, and she was walking too slowly."

"We could have taken turns carrying Sammy. He was

a hungry, tired baby who didn't understand what was happening. Mrs. Stewart has never forgiven you, and you forgot all about him!"

That day Sammy died rushes back to me. I remember the terror, the horror, and the grief as though he'd been murdered just that morning. What I remember most was my still silence, so afraid of doing or saying anything that might have made them angry enough to kill me. The meek little lamb. And now here I am scolding Grandfather as though he's family.

"You're so impatient, and you always expect the worst," I say.

"You're right," he replies softly.

In Fairfield I'd complain to my Aunt Orpah after my frequent quarrels with Dougal. "He's so lazy," I would shout, stamping my foot on her kitchen floor, "because he's always been the favorite."

"That's the trouble with families," she'd say, handing me a molasses cookie. "They're the people we know best, so we always think we know better."

I haven't scolded my family in months, I think in shock, not since the dead of winter. And why is that? Because I don't know them anymore.

Back home journeymen portrait painters travel from town to town, with canvases where the hair, hats, and clothes are already painted in. Only the faces are blank, nothing but bare cloth. The customer pays for his face, or the face of a loved one, to be painted on the canvas. Sometimes a favorite pet–a horse, cat, dog, or bird–is added for a personal touch and an extra payment.

The Campbells are like those faceless portraits. I remember our clothes, our livestock, and our gray and calico barn cats. But the faces of my parents, Dougal, Aunt Orpah, and Grandfather Campbell are a blur. I don't remember their features anymore.

I watch Grandfather stir the fire. He was afraid, I realize. He was afraid we would die if we didn't reach the Cuyahoga before the first snow. Sammy Stewart was a risk he couldn't afford to take.

He's my family, I think in amazement–along with Hepte, White Eyes, and Chickadee. These are the people I know best.

"I have given Mrs. Stewart a chance for more children and still she's angry. Four muskets." He shakes his head. "Not four muskets. Two. Maybe three. She would be happier with her own kind?"

"Of course."

"Good. Go to sleep."

"What about muskets?"

"Go to sleep, Nuxkwis. No more English."

As I doze off thinking about the muskets, I figure it out.

He wants to trade Mrs. Stewart to Sequin for muskets.

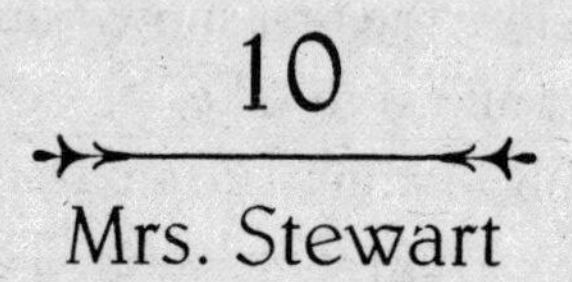

10

Mrs. Stewart

ABOUT A MONTH AFTER OUR TRIP TO SEQUIN'S, spring weather empties the cave. A war party leaves to explore the riverbanks, upstream and down. They are gone for days. Then one evening, just as the sun is dropping into the trees on the other side of the gorge, the men return to the cave, their voices full of relief and wonder: There are no other people on the river. We are safe from the Iroquois.

Chickadee and I find golden-yellow marsh marigolds in the thawing swamps. I teach her how to make garlands for our hair.

Once Grandfather is sure the winter is really over, we pack up all our belongings. The winter clothes and cooking pots, the knives and spoons, the muskets, the vegetable seeds, and the bearskin and wolfskin blankets are all tucked away into knapsacks and bags.

We have bright-red cloth for dresses and new copper kettles as shiny as pennies for cooking. The men look more relaxed now that they have plenty of shot and powder.

At last the bright-green leaves have a May look to them. I wonder if today is my birthday. If it is, that means I've been a captive for one year. On my last birthday, I lay in bed waiting to see what twelve felt like. That was only one year ago! After all that's happened, I feel as though one hundred years have passed, not just one.

When we have collected everything, we walk along the cliff trail. Instead of turning toward the river, we climb up the gorge to a flat piece of land just to the left of our cave. There's a stream winding through the center of the flat land. The water tumbles over the cliff to the river. This flat land above the cave will be our new home.

The men chop down the saplings and the women dig out the roots with shovels made of elk collarbones and flint knives. I help pile the sodden roots onto a steaming fire. Later we'll mix the root ashes back into the soil.

The men carefully peel the bark off the big trees and cut down more saplings. We all work together to make wigwams, twenty-five of them, one for each family. The bark is layered carefully over the springy saplings, then lashed together with grapevines.

Inside, our wigwam is almost as dark as the cave, but Hepte has covered the floor with pine needles. Sleeping on pine needles is a great comfort compared to the wet cave floor–the needles are soft and fill my nose with their crisp scent every time I move.

Our family fire is made up of five logs shaped into a star. Hepte calls it a starfire. I remember a woman on the march carrying live coals in a covered stone pot. Whenever we stopped, she added wood chips to the pot. Last fall, on the first night we spent in the cave, she added burning wood chips to each family's fire. Now she is going from starfire to starfire, adding more wood chips to each one.

When she comes to our starfire, Hepte looks pleased and relieved. I ask her to explain.

Hepte tells me, slowly, that our starfires should never stop burning or the wigwam will die along with everyone in it. In the first days none other than Kishelemukong himself, the Creator, allowed bits of stars to fall from the sky and ignite the flames.

She points to our fire. "Our Turtle clan starfire has been burning since those first days."

That can't be true, I think. "Since before the *yah-qua-whee* were killed?"

"Of course."

I shake my head. "No sense."

"In the first days," she says slowly, "a giant turtle rose from the sea, and the plants, the animals, and the People grew on his back. As long as there are the People and as long as their starfires burn, the giant turtle will float on the sea's surface and life will continue. If the fires go out, everything, even light itself, will disappear.

"The People honor turtles because of their patience and long life. Turtles can live on land and water. They feed on animals and plants. They can thrive anywhere."

That's why we're the Turtle clan, I think. It makes sense that the royal clan would be named after them.

"The Bear clan, the Wolf clan, the Turkey clan also honor turtles?" I ask.

"Yes."

"Grandfather is like the giant turtle. He holds up the world, or at least his part of it."

"I will tell him you said that," Hepte says with a smile.

I study our starfire as though it were a living thing. The flickering firelight does seem to whisper of ancient times and carefully guarded secrets. I wonder if these secrets will ever be told to me.

As I go to sleep, I remember that I haven't seen Mrs. Stewart today. It's been a long day; we hauled our baggage up the cliff trail, we built wigwams, the starfires are burning once more.

Where was Mrs. Stewart?

She must have been gathering firewood, I tell myself, or peeling bark for the wigwams. Maybe she's finally decided to work.

When the time comes to plant the seeds, the girls, women, and old men use elk-collarbone shovels to break up the earth. We sift the crisscrossed leftover roots out with our fingers and throw them into another steaming fire. The sun is hot, but the wet soil is cold, and by the end of the day my fingers are as cold and stiff as when I jumped into the Cuyahoga.

The gorge has turned lacy white with dogwood blossoms. Our winter birds–redbirds, chickadees, blue jays–must fight with the newcomers for tree space. Every day I see more and more springtime birds: golden finches, bluebirds, redwing blackbirds, scarlet tanagers, orioles, purple warblers. Their singing and bright feathers delight my ears and eyes. The robins hip-hop along the riverbank looking for worms, first with one eye cocked to the ground and then the other, as if they can't decide which eye works the better.

Hepte says it's planting time for the Three Sisters–the corn, the squash, and the beans. We'll also plant pumpkins. Each woman has brought her own supply of seeds on the long march from the Allegheny.

We plant the corn inside the circle of wigwams and on both sides of the stream. Once the cornstalks are knee high, the beans and squash will be planted. The cornstalks will serve as bean poles; their shadows will provide shade for the squash and pumpkin vines.

The vegetables' roots will nourish one another and the soil surrounding them.

"Like good sisters," Hepte tells me as Chickadee laughs and pats my face, "the vegetables help one another grow strong."

Hepte explains slowly and carefully; I understand just about everything she says. Chickadee is much harder to follow. She speaks too quickly, and her words blur together because she's lost her front baby teeth. White Eyes doesn't talk to me much; he spends most of his time with the men.

Grandfather has told everyone No English, so I've

had no choice but to learn their language. Most of the families are Unami, including mine, but there are other Delaware–a few Mohicans and Munsees–in our group. Just like me, they are all homesick for their lands and the way of life they left in the east.

All last winter Grandfather and a group of four other men met every few days to practice speaking English. I was always welcome. Now he shoos me away.

"Muxomsa, please," I plead with him. "My English will go."

"You will not forget. Your English is here." He taps my chest, where my heart beats underneath.

"We help each other? I help with hard words."

"I already know the hard words. Nuxkwis, you help us more by speaking only Unami." He turns his back and refuses to discuss the English-talking group again.

"Grandfather is as mean as a bear," I say to Hepte that afternoon in our garden. "I am afraid to lose my English."

"You won't forget your English because it is nestled in your heart. You help us more if you learn Unami. My father is a wise man–you must listen to him. He is not only your grandfather but your sachem as well."

I look at her suspiciously. Has she been talking to him about me?

"Think about everything you have learned just by listening hard and asking questions."

"*Heh-heh,*" I mutter, throwing a tangle of roots onto the fire.

No time like the present, I think as I clear my throat. "I need to talk to Mrs. Stewart. Important."

"If Mrs. Stewart wants to spend the rest of her days living in the cave, then let her," Hepte says hotly.

"But I care–"

"I don't care. We don't care. You don't care. Understand?" Hepte looks at me, and I see the same flashing anger in her eyes as I see in her father's sometimes.

She turns away to shake soil from a mass of roots.

I'm working hard this afternoon, and the sun is hot. We're wearing just leather aprons. I have an idea for getting away and warning Mrs. Stewart.

"Hepte." I point to my milk-white chest and back. "I am thinking, the sun will cook me? Um . . . red me?"

"Tonn . . ." Hepte smiles. "We get sunburned too."

"The sun is too strong for me. I will stoke the starfire. Please, *Gahes*?"

Gahes.

I've never called her "mother" before.

I have trouble meeting her eyes, but when I do, I see Hepte looking at me with her own eyes wet and shining.

"Tonn," she whispers, "you may leave our garden."

I run back to the wigwam and pull my cotton dress over my shoulders. When I'm sure no one is looking, I climb down the cliff path to the cave.

Guilt tweaks at my heart because I lied to Hepte and called her "mother." She has treated me with nothing but kindness, often giving me food when she has none. But I can't let them trade Mrs. Stewart to that grimy Sequin as though she were a doeskin or a beaver pelt. If

I warn her, she'll come out of the cave and work, earn her keep. Then Grandfather won't trade her for muskets.

At first I see no one in the cave. When my eyes adjust to the dimness, I see a figure in the corner holding a bundle in her arms. A bad sign.

She's sitting by what was once a fire. Now there's nothing but cinders and ashes.

"Mrs. Stewart, I've come to warn you."

She looks up in alarm and holds the bundle closer to her. When she sees it's me, her shoulders relax.

"Mary! Sit down next to the fire. This is a rare surprise."

The bundle is a short log wrapped in deerskin. I know what it's supposed to be–she's been holding it off and on all winter.

"You're holding Sammy again, Mrs. Stewart. You told me you wouldn't do that anymore."

She presses her thin cheek to the bark and rocks it back and forth. Her eyes are bright with fear as she whispers to the log.

"Listen carefully. I don't have much time–I'm supposed to be tending our fire. Netawatwees Sachem wants to trade you to Sequin for muskets."

She tilts her head slightly in my direction. "Sequin? Muskets? Trade?"

"That filthy little Frenchman with the trading post by Cat Lake, the Erie Lake. He wants to trade muskets for a wife." I don't tell her that he's already tried trading muskets for me.

"Grandfather wants to trade you for muskets because you won't work. They can't afford to keep anyone who won't work. So you have to leave the cave and tend the garden. You have to leave *now*."

I brace myself for her anger, her outrage.

Instead, Mrs. Stewart looks at the bundle for a long time. At first I think she doesn't understand what I said to her. She has that same hollow look in her eyes I saw in the weeks after our capture.

"What does Mr. Sequin's cabin look like, Mary?"

"It's disgusting. The trading-post side isn't so bad, but the side where he lives! Dirty clothes, smelly linens, and cook pots so filthy, there's mold growing out of them."

"Furniture?"

"Lots of furniture. Fancy things–hand carved, I mean. He must have portaged it down the St. Lawrence from Montreal, or France even. But the furniture's spoiled too."

"Fancy things," Mrs. Stewart echoes. "I had to sell my mother's mahogany sideboard before our removal to Pennsylvania."

After living for so long with people who don't speak English, I've learned to read faces. Mrs. Stewart's face is full of hope–hope and escape.

"I can't believe what you're thinking! You're . . . you're already married," I stammer. Married to two husbands, I almost say, but I catch myself in time.

"Am I?" she says softly.

"You haven't even asked me what Sequin looks like."

"I don't care what he looks like," she says in a dreamy voice. "I want a good home, for Sammy and me."

"You'll have to kiss him," I reply hotly. "And he hasn't even got teeth."

"Have I ever told you that my name is Mary too?"

"No." I hesitate for a moment. "But you can't–"

"My name is Mary Stewart," she says softly. "And any life is better than this one. I have no hope, Mary, don't you see?"

Down in the gorge a blue heron flaps out of a huge nest high in a treetop. I watch her as she glides just above the Cuyahoga, looking for fish for her babies.

"He has soap," I finally say. "Soap that smells like roses. Not that he's ever used any."

"Hope," Mrs. Stewart says softly, or maybe she says "Soap." She takes a deep breath and holds the bundle closer to her. "Tell that high-and-mighty old Netawatwees I'll go to Sequin's. Tell him Sammy and I will leave today."

"Oh no! If I tell him you want to go, he'll know I've been talking to you."

"I don't understand your meaning, Mary."

"Grandfather won't let me speak English anymore. I'm not allowed. I'm not supposed to be in the cave talking to you."

She grasps my elbow. "What do you mean he won't let you speak English?"

Her red, wrinkled hand looks like a turkey buzzard's claw. It's all I can do not to pull away from her. "He says I have to learn their language."

"You're turning into a savage, right in front of my eyes! Come with me," she says, giving my elbow a little pull. "Sequin will want you, too."

"NO!" I shout. "I can't. The . . . the Turtles would never let me leave. You'll have to speak for yourself, Mrs. Stewart. Talk to Netawatwees Sachem yourself."

"Mary," Mrs. Stewart says in a bewildered voice, "what do turtles have to do with your leaving?"

"It's their name, I reckon: Hepte, Chickadee, Grandfather."

Mrs. Stewart shakes her head and clutches the log closer.

"We'll have to talk to him together then," I say. "He'll be angry with me, but he'll be gladder still to be rid of you, especially if it means muskets."

I've never heard Mrs. Stewart laugh before. Her lilting, feminine laughter bounces off the walls of the cave.

Back in Fairfield we used to have a festive Saturday-night supper before Christmas week with hymn singing afterward.

Just hearing Mrs. Stewart's laughter makes me smell again the pine and holly boughs on the walls, and the hams, spicy pies, and rich cakes on my mother's sideboards.

We'd invite all our friends and relations. At our party I would sit on the staircase with Constance, studying the pretty young women of the town. They would laugh just like that, standing in the center of a flock of admirers. The bright fans they fluttered in front of their smiles shimmered like butterfly wings.

When we walk into our village above the cave, the Turtle, the Turkey, the Wolf, and the Bear clans stop and stare at Mrs. Stewart. She is still wearing the red dress she was wearing when we were captured, except now her blackened knees poke out between shreds of stained cloth. Her hair is stuck together in a gray clump like a horse's hoof. She is cradling her bundled log and blinking as an owl does in the sunlight.

As we approach the English-talking group, they stop speaking one by one. No one likes Mrs. Stewart, but now they look at her in horror and pity. Other people crowd behind us, their faces watchful and waiting.

"Muxomsa," I say softly, looking at my feet, "Mrs. Stewart says she goes to Sequin by the Erie Lake. Two muskets? Maybe three? If she washes and has new clothes."

"She looks like a crazy woman," Grandfather shouts. "Sequin will trade muskets for a bitter, crazy woman?"

"Not bitter. Not crazy. She wants to leave. This sun."

Hepte says, "Father, I have made a new dress with Sequin's red cloth. She may have the new dress if you bring more cloth back, enough cloth for your granddaughters and myself."

"More cloth and muskets for this?" Grandfather flings an arm in Mrs. Stewart's direction.

Mrs. Stewart steps forward. "Netawatwees, I don't understand what you're saying, but I hear the scorn in your voice. Not that I've ever given a fig as to what your opinion is of me. I want to go. I want to leave."

Grandfather switches to English. "Then leave. Today," he says angrily. "My daughter has offered a dress. My granddaughter will help you wash–"

Oh, no I won't. Just the thought of touching that filthy, clumped hair makes my skin crawl.

"–and when you're ready my son-in-law will take you to Sequin's."

"On one condition. Apparently, Mary disobeyed you in coming to the cave and speaking to me. She came to help. You're not to punish her for that."

My mouth drops open. This is Mrs. Stewart?

Grandfather and Mrs. Stewart stare hard into each other's eyes. He blinks first.

"No punishment," he mutters.

"Regular visits, too. I'll not abandon her to you."

Grandfather gives her a short nod. "Hepte will come down the cliff trail with the dress."

"Good-bye, Netawatwees."

Grandfather puts his hand out as though he expects her to shake it. Instead, Mrs. Stewart turns slowly on her cracked heels. When did she lose her shoes?

Her head is held high. With her back as straight as a ramrod, she walks faster and faster down the rows of wigwams toward the cliff trail. I have to trot to keep up.

Finally I stop as she begins her descent.

"I'll miss you," I call out to her. "Thank you for . . . helping me. Good-bye." I wave my hand, but she doesn't look back.

"Good-bye, Mary Stewart," I whisper.

Mrs. Stewart breaks into a run and disappears down the cliff trail.

11

Questions

MRS. STEWART HAS BEEN GONE FOR WEEKS. Once more the little presents from Kolachuisen appear at my shoulder every morning. Each daybreak I awake to a pretty leaf, or a trim milkweed pod with a stem leaking sap, or a pebble the same dainty pink as my fingernails after an afternoon spent scrubbing pots in the river. Once there was a crisp strip of birch bark crafted into a tiny canoe.

This morning I found three tiny blueberries nestled in an acorn cap.

Every breakfast Kolachuisen watches me eat with the Turtle clan. She always finds a way to work next to me in the gardens. She follows me when I gather wood. Her family wigwam is close to ours. In the evening, whenever I talk to Hepte, or Chickadee, or Grandfather, out of the corner of my eye I see Kolachuisen watching me and listening to what I say.

I lie awake at night, considering what to do. I haven't talked to someone my own age since leaving Fairfield. I wonder if I've forgotten how to talk to another girl. I wonder if I've forgotten what to talk about.

Constance and I swore we'd be best friends forever, but surely she's made another best friend by now. That doesn't mean she's forgotten me; I haven't forgotten her. It would be grand to share secrets with someone again. As I watch our starfire wane to embers, I decide to be Kolachuisen's friend.

Today, while gathering wood, I nod and smile to her, and it's as though I've tapped a keg of cider. The words flow out and don't stop.

"Do you like it here?" she says as she wrinkles her nose. "I hate the Oyo Hoking. I wish we hadn't left the Allegheny. There aren't enough people here. It's too lonesome.

"Did you know Buckahelagas snores in his sleep? Every night last winter I listened to him snore, just like a bear in a cave, and thought, 'This is my future husband? This is the boy my parents want me to marry? I have to listen to that snore every night for the rest of my life?'"

She giggles and looks over her shoulder.

"I wouldn't mind listening to Makiawip snore for the rest of my life–don't you think he's handsome? I'm sure I've seen him looking at me."

She kicks a tree root and scowls.

"But he's been promised to Tankawon, but I don't think she's very pretty. Do you? She's got that long nose, just like an opossum's nose."

She wiggles her nose, then lowers her voice. "Tankawon is only Turkey clan–what were Makiawip's parents thinking? And–"

"Kolachuisen," I break in. "Please. Too many words. My head will hurt."

She looks crushed. "It has been such a long time since I had someone to talk to. I was waiting for you to learn our language and . . . to be happy again. So we could be friends."

"We can be friends. I think Makiawip is handsome, too." I take her hand. "Thank you for the presents. I have so many questions."

She smiles again. "We can talk all the time now. So," she leans forward and whispers, "who do you want to marry?"

"What?"

"You're twelve winters, aren't you? Just like me? In two more winters you'll be married."

"I–I will?" I stammer. My knees collapse under me and I land hard on the gorge's steep slope. Kolachuisen sits next to me.

"If you don't choose someone, they'll choose him for you, so you'd better start looking," she says in a low voice. "Not that we've got much to choose from around here. Maybe more Delaware will come here next summer. Or maybe we'll have Wyandot or Shawnee husbands."

"A Shawnee husband," I whisper. My blood runs cold just thinking about it.

But I'll be long gone before I'm fourteen. I'll be rescued and back in Pennsylvania. Won't I?

Won't I?

My heart starts to pound. What if I am married when the king's men come to rescue me? I hadn't thought of that. Could I leave a husband behind? Or my own *children*? Surely I couldn't be like Mrs. Stewart, replacing one family with another without even a look backward?

All my life I've heard of captives who refused to return to the settlements. Their white families are their past, their new families are their future.

Is this my life to come? A Delaware husband, wigwams, leather clothes, and heathen children who won't look anything like me?

What if I brought my new family to Campbell Station with me? I try to imagine the Campbells with a Delaware son-in-law and half-breed grandchildren. My parents sit at table with their faces turned to the wall. My children cry and ask to be taken home. I tell them home is your family.

Only Dougal makes them feel welcome. He thinks it's grand having a brother who's an Indian.

So as not to suffer the same fate as Sammy Stewart, I tried to divide myself into two Marys. The meek and mild lamb Mary was the only Mary the Delaware would ever see. The real Mary I'd keep hidden away until I saw the Campbells again.

As it turns out, the Delaware like the real Mary better. So do I, I reckon. Lambs are sweet and gentle but boring, to tell the truth.

But it's all so confusing–the true and the false, the real and the lamb. Does the true Mary or the false Mary wait to be rescued? Does the real Mary or the lamb Mary consider marriage with a Delaware or even a Shawnee?

"Mary." Kolachuisen pinches my arm. "You weren't listening."

"Kolachuisen." How do I tell her my mind was a thousand miles away? Or at the very least in Pennyslvania? "I have never thought about being married."

"You haven't?" she shouts.

"No! I mean . . . I have never thought about marriage among the Delaware." I look at her. "I don't think about the time to come very often."

She doesn't say anything but looks at me with narrowed eyes. I decide to change the subject.

"Kolachuisen, why are there no girls our age among us? Tell me about Netawatwees Sachem's older granddaughter. How many winters was she? What was she like? No one in the Turtle clan talks about her. Did she do something wrong?"

Kolachuisen jumps to her feet. She looks terrified. "We never talk about them," she says, shaking her head.

"*Keko windji?*" I ask. "Kolachuisen?"

But she's already slip-sliding down the gorge toward the river trail.

That evening, as the Turtle clan talks around me, my mind feels on fire with questions. Except for my rescue, I haven't given my future much thought–my life as a grown woman, I mean. What if I'm not rescued? Just who will Mary Caroline Campbell be then? I'm certainly not a Delaware, but I scarcely remember being a Campbell anymore either. Who am I?

I'm in the middle and I've never felt so alone.

White Eyes and Grandfather have made us a summer porch on the southern side of our wigwam, the side that always faces the sun. It's pleasant sitting here, especially of an evening, watching the sun set and the moon wax and wane, rise and fall.

I stay awake tonight as Grandfather, White Eyes, and Chickadee enter the wigwam and nod off to sleep. Hepte is awake, as always. She's always the last one to retire at night and the first one to awaken in the morning.

"Tonn," she says, "you are quiet this evening."

"Hepte," I say cautiously, "I have many questions. Why are Kolachuisen and I the only girls of twelve winters?"

"A sickness came," she says, so softly at first, I thought I heard the wind whispering through the pines instead of her voice. "And the others a few winters more than you are already married. They are no longer girls."

"Kolachuisen was talking today about marriage."

She laughs. "Kolachuisen likes to talk."

"She says I will be married soon."

"You want to be married?"

"Someday," I answer anxiously, "but I hope not soon." I hold my breath, waiting to hear what plans the Turtle clan has for me.

Hepte nods. "Not soon. You have a long time before marriage."

My breath gushes out all at once. "I am glad to hear you say that."

Hepte is pulling a rabbit skin to soften it. She pulls and pulls for a long time. I've noticed that her hands never stop moving: stirring stewpots, planting seeds, tanning hides, sewing, braiding hair, scrubbing clothes, sweeping. Her hands are as thickly muscled as a man's.

She asks, "You have another question?"

"Please tell me about your daughter," I say softly.

"Her real name is Wapashuiwi. That's a small white wildcat with fur on the tips of her ears."

"White Lynx," I think in English. I'll ask Grandfather if that's right.

Hepte says, "But it was you who started calling her Chickadee. Her new name suits her. Everyone calls her Chickadee now."

"No, I mean your other daughter."

"I should talk about you?" Hepte asks playfully.

I don't know their word for "dead." I've never heard anyone say it. "No, I mean the daughter who first had the moccasins."

"We never talk about them," Hepte says quickly.

"But why won't you talk about her? What did she do that was so bad?"

Hepte looks startled. "She did nothing wrong. We don't talk about those who are no longer with us."

"Did she look like me? What was her name? If I am to replace her, I must know about her."

"You do replace her," Hepte says softly. "You are a fine daughter. It is time to go to sleep."

"You can tell me nothing about her?" I ask. "Her name? How many winters she had? Anything?"

Hepte takes my chin in her hands and looks into my eyes. "You do replace her. You have replaced her in all our hearts."

"You've forgotten her?"

"Of course we will never forget her. But you have filled that empty place she left in our hearts."

"Please tell me something about her. Please. Everyone else knew her. I need to know something about her."

It's hard to explain, but if I can learn something important about her, I know I'll learn something important about me.

Hepte puts her hands in her lap. "I will tell you these things," she replies. "She was your grandfather's first grandchild. He loved her very much! When he looked at her, there was so much love in his face. Sometimes I see that same look on his face when he looks at you.

"She is there." Hepte points to the Milky Way high above our heads. "Those stars make up the pathway of souls, on their way to Heaven."

"Your mother is up there, too?" I ask shyly.

"Yes. They are together as we are together."

"What I have learned tonight has lightened my heart. I was feeling so alone today, so . . . in the middle. I no longer have this feeling. Thank you for telling me about her. Good night, Hepte."

She looks at me askance. "Won't you call me Gahes? The one and only time you called me that, you wanted to gain favor to see Mrs. Stewart."

She looks at me expectantly.

I can call her Gahes. She's done so much for me, I can do

this for her, to make her happy. They're not even the same words, gahes *and "mother," so I won't be disloyal to my own mother.*

"Ga . . . ga," I say before dissolving into tears.

"You must love her very much," Hepte says, "and miss her."

"More," I sob, "more than she loves me."

Hepte says as she puts her arm around me, "No daughter loves her mother more than her mother loves her. Now go to sleep."

The next evening all the men sit glumly together. The man who had been carrying all the gunpowder in a knapsack tripped into the river. The gunpowder sank to the river bottom. The Winter Moon boys eagerly jumped in after it, keen to show off their strength and swimming prowess. No one came ashore with the knapsack.

The men will have to go back to Sequin's trading post for more gunpowder. I beg Grandfather for a chance to go with them.

"Muxomsa," I say, "I wish to see Mrs. Stewart."

He shakes his head in exasperation. "Why do you want to see that angry, bitter woman?"

"Please. I want to see if she's happy."

"And if she's not?"

"Tonn," Hepte says, "Sequin will see you again. Perhaps he will think he did not get such a good trade for his muskets after all. He will be angry and raise his prices."

"Muxomsa, please."

"Do not think about her," he orders, waving his hand impatiently. "Talk of something else."

"The gunpowder, then. This morning, after the powder sank into the river, we wanted to know what happened, in the same way we want to know the end of a story. What happened to Mrs. Stewart is like not knowing the end of a story.

"I don't know the word in Unami, but in English it's *curious.* Do you know this word, Muxomsa?"

"I know this word. You are sure that is all? Only *curious*?"

"Yes," I reply.

"Mrs. Stewart is the sort of person who is never happy. We gave her a new home, a new husband, a chance for new children. But still she was not happy. We should never have taken her, or we should have killed her along the way."

I think about all the times I cried myself to sleep when I was first captured. "Would you have killed me?" I ask him breathlessly.

"We talked about it."

"Father," Hepte scolds, then turns to me. "You are a good daughter and very pretty. We are worried Sequin will want you for himself."

"But if Sequin is happy with Mrs. Stewart, he will not raise his prices. He may even lower them. Please, Grandfather. You need a woman to carry food."

He gazes thoughtfully into the fire. I hold my breath and wait for him to decide.

"You may go with us."

I let out my breath. "May I speak English with Mrs. Stewart?"

"You may speak English with Mrs. Stewart. But if she is not happy, that is the end of it."

12

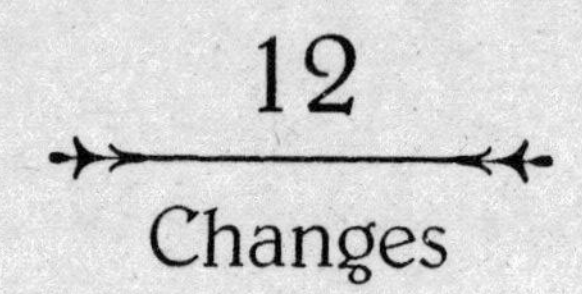

Changes

THREE DAYS LATER WE LEAVE for Sequin's trading post. Hepte tells me to wash my face and hands in the river before seeing Mrs. Stewart. She tells me twice, then reminds me again. I think she doesn't want Mrs. Stewart to see me with dirty hands and a dirty face. Hepte doesn't want Mrs. Stewart to think that she hasn't been taking care of me.

Before we leave, Chickadee rushes out of the wigwam with my doll clutched in her fist.

"She will be lonely," she says, pressing the doll into my hand.

"Kamis Chickadee, you keep her for me."

When I give the doll back, Chickadee's eyes sparkle as she holds it close to her cheek.

We walk down the cliff trail and follow the river path north to Sequin's.

The leaves look like early September–that bright, solid green with touches of gold at the tips. The morning air has a snap to it; the evenings are wondrously clear. Little sassafras plants cover the forest floor. In the greenish sunlight we see deer and fawns grazing in the glades. When they see us, they bound away in fear, the mothers' white tails flashing between the trees like dogwood blossoms caught in a breeze.

We stop for a swim in a calm part of the Cuyahoga. The cold water feels good on my hot head and neck.

I am the last one out of the river. The men are anxious to leave. They scowl and complain that I am taking too long to dress; it will be dark soon, and we have a long way to go before then. I tell them it's hard tying thongs and squeezing into a too-small tunic. They just complain more. No one offers to help.

These men remind me of my father Campbell–distant, separate, and always in a hurry, with important things to do before dark.

Walking along the river this time, I notice funny-looking hills. They're not very big–thirty feet tall, I reckon. I could walk around one in a minute or two. The hills are always in groups of three or more. They're well away from the river, but not so far away that I can't see them in the leafy distance.

"Muxomsa." I point to them. "Odd-looking hills."

"Not hills exactly. Mounds. Ancient ones we call the Talega buried their dead in these mounds along with jewelry, weapons, cooking pots: things they would need for the next world. The bigger the mound, the more important the person.

"In ancient times, we Delaware were known as Lenape. We Lenape fought bitter wars with the Talega. We fought for possession of the Oyo Hoking. The Talega won these wars, so we had no choice but to move farther east. Now here we are in the Oyo Hoking, and the Talega are long gone."

"The Talega are still in the mounds?" I ask. "Their bones? They were here when the *yah-qua-whee* were here?"

"Perhaps."

The next time we walk past a group of mounds, I run over and press my hands against one. Small trees jut out at odd angles. The bottom of the mound is honeycombed with burrows, probably woodchuck or maybe even badger. I peer into the biggest burrow, looking for the gleam of human bone.

"You saw the elephants," I whisper to the ancient bones in English. "What were you thinking, when you saw the elephants?"

It is early afternoon on the third day when we reach Sequin's trading post. The first surprise is a cow in the front yard. Her front legs are hobbled together and she is placidly munching grass. She looks up in a bored sort of way as we step onto the porch.

We enter the trading post. At first I can only stare, my mouth open so wide, my jaw feels as though it could bang against my knees. Everything is as neat as a pin. The floor is swept. The copper cooking pots catch the firelight and shimmer from their hooks above the fireplace. No more smelly linens line the walls. The floor is no longer crusty with wads of dried chewing tobacco.

The fancy French furniture is shiny with wax, and the spotless windows and mirrors sparkle in the sunlight. I stare hard at the windows. Lace curtains!

Something delicious bubbles in a pot hanging in the fireplace. Steaming loaves of bread rest on the table, half hidden in linen napkins. The smell of freshly baked bread is like heaven and sets my mouth a-watering. A pretty woman in a lacy pink dress turns away from her cooking to look at us.

"Mary! This is a rare surprise. So good of you to call."

"Mrs. Stewart?" I exclaim.

"Oh no, don't call me that, honey," she says quickly. She rushes over to us and kisses me on the cheek.

"You smell like ro-roses," I stammer. "Like the soap."

"Call me Mrs. Sequin," she whispers in my ear. "Let me look at you, Mary."

While she looks at me, I gape at her. Her blue eyes sparkle under blond, curly hair caught up in an elegant tortoiseshell comb. The lacy pink dress she's wearing is exactly the same color as the blush in her cheeks. She's smiling and happier than I've ever seen her, even when we knew each other back in Pennsylvania.

"How pretty you are, Mary," she says to me. "You're growing up into a very pretty young woman. Your mother would be so pleased."

Next to her frillery I feel shabby in my deerskin dress, leggings, and moccasins. My hair is coming loose from its braids and my skin is as brown as the deerskin. I feel hot and sticky, and my clothes smell like smoke.

"You look so–so different," I stammer, "in your fancy French frippery." I glance at Grandfather and the other men. They're staring at Mrs. Stewart in amazement, too.

Mrs. Stewart draws herself up tall and looks Grandfather right in the eyes. She pulls me to her and draws her arm around my shoulder.

"Netawatwees," she says stiffly, "my husband is on the porch." She turns her head and shouts, "François!" in a voice so loud we all jump. "Customers! *François!*"

Sequin scurries through the porch door, and now we all stare at him. His bear-fur hair is pulled back, and his beard is gone. Instead of greasy buckskin he's wearing a spotless shirt and breeches. And wonder of wonders, clean hose and shoes!

Mrs. Stewart gives him a sharp look, and he hurries over to the counter. He glances at me, then quickly looks away.

"While the men are at their business, let's go outside, Mary. Have you seen our lake view? It's really quite charming."

Mrs. Stewart lifts a rose-colored parasol from a shelf full of merchandise, and we step onto the porch.

We walk along the beach, and the breeze off the lake feels cool and fresh. The water is a clear and delicate bluish-green that reminds me of the glass candy jars on Sequin's counter.

"Grandfather said I could come with him to see you. I told him I wanted to make sure you were happy."

Mrs. Stewart doesn't say anything. She uses the parasol to shade her face as she picks her way delicately over sand as white as sugar. She dodges the waves in little calfskin boots. I kick off my moccasins and let the waves wash over my feet. The water is cold and refreshing. Seaweed tangles around my ankles. I pick up shells with my toes.

"He said happy or not, I should forget about you," I say.

Mrs. Stewart scowls. "That sounds like old high-and-mighty Netawatwees, doesn't it?"

"He's their king, Mrs. Stewart. I've never met anyone so wise. He even went to a boys' school in Philadelphia."

She sighs and draws me close to her. "Call me Mrs. Sequin, Mary. Or Madame Sequin."

I wipe the sweat from my brow with my sleeve. "Mrs. Sequin. Have you ever gone swimming in the Erie Lake?"

"Swimming!" She studies my face. "You're turning into a little Indian, Mary. Your skin is as brown as a little Indian's."

"I've been working in our garden. You must have had a kitchen garden, back in New Jersey or Pennsylvania."

Mrs. Sequin looks at the waves rolling toward the beach. She has a peculiar look on her face, and now I'm sorry I mentioned her kitchen garden. Surely she doesn't want to remember home anymore.

"I'm happy, Mary, but it's a different kind of happiness. Sometimes I awaken in the morning thinking, I can't believe this is my life. How did I ever acquire the strength to live this life? But the strength is here, within me. Perhaps it's always been there."

"Maybe the strength we need is the strength we have," I reply.

"What a curious thing to say, Mary. I'll tell you a secret. Not even François knows. I'm going to have a baby next winter. I'm going to name it Samuel or Samantha, in remembrance of little Sammy. He never even had the chance to make his mark in the world. I can't think of anything sadder than that."

"I remember him." I don't tell her that what I remember is endless crying and fussing.

She gives me another kiss. "Of course you do, honey."

"Where did you get all these pretty things?"

"François is not just a shopkeeper, Mary. He's more like . . . an ambassador, the French ambassador to these people. This dress and a dozen more were packed away in trunks, can you imagine? Frocks from Paris! Of course Indian women wouldn't appreciate real French dresses. But I appreciate them."

She's taken over his shop, I think. *Things he's supposed to be selling she took for herself.*

"The cow?" I ask.

"She's been here since early summer. A gift from the Governor of Montreal–Pierre de Rigaud, Marquis de Vaudreuil-Cavagnal."

She rattles the name off her tongue so easily that I know she's been practicing.

"There've been some big changes, Mary. Last September, while we were on the march to the

Cuyahoga, General Marquis de Montcalm surrendered to General Wolfe on the Plains of Abraham near Quebec City. Do you know what that means?"

I shake my head.

"It means the war is over and the French have lost! They surrendered Canada to England. All of Canada is ours now.

"The French are thinking of their lands in the west. The Governor presented us with an exquisite set of china and silver, too, once he learned of Mr. Sequin's marriage."

I almost blurt out, "He got married?" but I catch myself just in time.

"The Governor is hoping this trading post will show that they have a stronger claim in this heathen wilderness than the British."

"But Ohio is British land, isn't it? Someday the king's men will come here and rescue us."

When she looks at the lake again, her parasol ruffles and lifts in the stiff breeze.

Succotash is a mixture of corn and beans, but I've always eaten around the beans, no matter how hungry I am. A rescue would be like a bowl of succotash–the corn and the beans, the good and the bad mixed together.

What would I do, I wonder, if I were to turn around right now and see soldiers standing on the beach behind me? They would say, "We've come to rescue you. At your service, Miss Campbell," and then they would bow at the waist.

I'd go with the soldiers. Of course I would. I don't really belong here.

Then I think of Chickadee's face, lit up with delight when I gave her my doll.

"I don't know whose land this is, Mary. It's all so confusing. When was the last time you had a glass of milk?"

"A long time ago."

"Stay for dinner. All of you. I'll have a dinner party tonight in your honor. But I allow only English to be spoken in my house. No French and none of that awful Indian jabber."

"A dinner party," I exclaim. "Perchance, do you have a tea called Pekoe? My mother used to brew that tea on special occasions."

She smiles at me. "I, too, have Pekoe for special occasions."

"Do you believe Satan lives . . . here in Ohio, I mean?" I blurt out. "That we're being tempted here in the wilderness?"

Mrs. Stewart takes my arm. "Do you feel tempted, Mary?"

"I feel befuddled, confused," I reply. "If we were rescued here, today, I'd think fondly on the Turtles for the rest of my life.

"I know they're heathen, they worship strange gods and believe a turtle is holding up the earth, instead of God's grace. I know they're evil, because of what they did to us. And Sammy.

"But I feel closer to them than my own family. How can that be? Confusion *is* temptation, isn't it? 'A befuddled mind invites temptation.' That's what Pastor Mainwood taught me."

She looks at me for a long time before answering. "Forbidden fruit doesn't always look like an apple, Mary. It can look like an Indian dress or forgetting to say your prayers at night. It can look like deliberately turning away from who you are."

"Mrs. Stewart, do you believe we'll be rescued someday? Really, really believe it?"

She cups her hand around my chin. "I've never stopped believing."

"I don't want to forget who I am. I haven't forgotten my evening prayers." Not that I think God listens anymore.

Mrs. Stewart–I mean Mrs. Sequin–looks at me with her hands folded across her chest and her eyebrows raised. "I'm going to insist that you stay with us. What would your mother think of me, knowing I left you to the heathens?"

I say all at once, "I can't stay here. Sequin wanted me in trade for muskets. Grandfather traded you instead."

Her face drains of color as she stares at me in shock. An eyeblink later she's patting her hair in place and smoothing her silk skirt.

"I didn't want to tell you," I whisper. "I'm sorry."

"Nonsense," she says briskly. "We'll have tea after your bathe and I'll fix your hair right pretty for my dinner party."

"You don't mind if I swim?"

"Bathing, Mary. I'll fetch you some soap. Bathing is another thing altogether."

After Mrs. Sequin goes back inside, I leave all my clothes on the beach. As I'm jumping into the crashing waves, I notice that I really am as brown all over as a Delaware.

Mrs. Sequin watches me from the back door. I wave to her and she waves back, but her face is angry and sad, as though she's lost something precious and doesn't know where to find it.

Sequin sits at the head of the table and Mrs. Sequin sits at the foot. We dine on mushroom, scallion, and cream soup; fresh roasted trout; and warm bread with real butter and blueberry jam. We eat venison steaks, potatoes, and carrots glazed in molasses. There's black-walnut apple cake and cream for dessert, with Pekoe tea.

Everything's so delicious, I can't stop eating.

I can't stop staring at the china plates, either, painted with pretty ladies wearing pink dresses and holding blue flowers. The silverware is heavy in my hands. A silver tea service gleams on the sideboard. White linen napkins grace each place setting. Delicate crystal goblets, two for each guest, hold real French wine (I'm having milk) and water.

A silver candelabrum lit with snow-white candles is the centerpiece. I doubt if our late Queen Caroline herself would have dined this elegantly.

Mrs. Sequin is glowing, she's so happy.

The Governor of Montreal is a smart man, I realize suddenly. Sequin has a face that could freeze July, but if his wife wants to think she's the wife of an ambassador (and have all the riches that come with it), she won't make him leave the wilderness and go back home. And that does give the French a keen advantage over the British here.

I try to remember my best dinner-party manners: elbows in, back straight and not touching the chair back, left hand in my lap. I dab a smooth-as-cream linen napkin against my lips. I remember to speak only when spoken to.

That part's easy, because I'm so embarrassed about my clothes. I didn't think to pack my new cloth dress. My deerskin dress is itchy from the beach sand, and it pinches around my shoulders and hips. My leggings have holes in the knees.

I'm also struck dumb by all the finery, absolutely tongue-tied. Every time I drink from one of my goblets, I'm afraid I'll break off a piece with my teeth. They look as fragile as eggshells. I'm afraid to reach for the saltcellar, for fear I'll knock over a candlestick and set fire to the French-linen tablecloth.

Mrs. Stewart tries to engage me in dinner-table talk about the weather, but all I can do is eat and stare. She's piled up my hair with lots of loops and curls, and my head feels heavy and stiff. The hairpins jab into my scalp. I had forgotten how much work it is to be beautiful.

I have nothing to say to her–nothing I can say in front of Grandfather, anyway. There are so many forbidden topics: Pennsylvania, Connecticut, Sammy, the new baby, Mr. Sequin, me with the Turtle clan and not with her and why.

All of a sudden her easy happiness makes me angry. It's an insult to Grandfather's long months of protection. It wasn't his fault we had to come to Ohio and spend the winter in a cave. It wasn't his fault there was never enough food. He did the best he could.

She hasn't even looked at Sequin all night, much less talked to him. All she wants is the comfort and luxury he can provide.

Sequin eats slowly and silently. Head bowed, he seems to have shrunk within himself, and he drinks glass after glass of wine.

I have always thought Mrs. Stewart and I were the same, that we were miserable in the wilderness for the same reasons. We're not the same at all. Now that she has replaced the things she left behind with new things, she's happy again.

Of course I miss things–our neighbor's sleigh, toasty hearthstones on winter nights, good food, my soft Connecticut bed.

But I miss the people far more than any of the things. I miss the way my grandfather Campbell called me "Marrah," as though he had a burr stuck in his throat. I miss Friday bake days with my aunt Orpah. In the depths of winter Constance and I would skate on Long Island Sound, sometimes as far as Fayerweather Island and back. And of course I miss my parents and my brother.

Things are replaceable, people are not.

So what are you doing here, Mary? You were taken captive a year ago to replace a daughter who'd died. They've accepted you as her. You're wrong. People are replaceable.

Replaceable maybe, but not forgotten, never forgotten.

I sleep by the fire on a red-satin couch in wondrous comfort. Mrs. Stewart's sharp whisper wakes me up.

"How could you even think such a thing? She's a child, she's a baby."

"Madame." Sequin says something so quick and throaty that I'm not sure whether it's French or English.

"You're a filthy, filthy people–"

"Madame–"

"Worse than the savages, worse."

"Madame, this baby as you say, you will awaken her."

The blankets rustle as Mrs. Sequin turns over and punches her pillow. "Filthy."

13

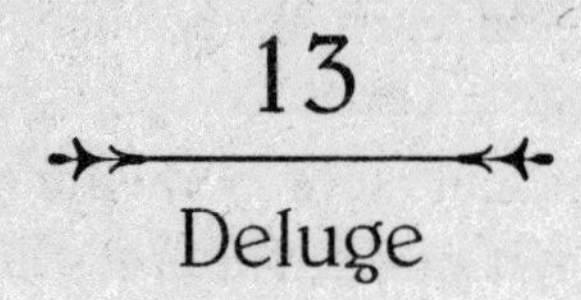

Deluge

OUR GARDENS ARE DOING WELL; the cornstalks are almost as tall as my chin. My father used to say the corn should be knee high by the first of July, so the summer must be almost over. At any rate, it feels like late summer.

Now that I've lost track of the days, I have to use other ways to mark the passing of time. The shrill singing of the tree frogs ends a little earlier each evening. Raccoons and woodchucks are out in the middle of the day, shamelessly stuffing themselves with anything they can find–mussels, acorns, blackberries, milky-green gooseberries–to fatten up for the long winter to come. The shadows stretch just a little longer than before. The days are still hot and sticky, but the nights are cooler.

The poison ivy winding around the oaks and black-walnut trees is turning scarlet. That means late August or early September back in Connecticut. I've been with Grandfather, Hepte, White Eyes, and Chickadee for more than a year.

Our pumpkins and squash are about the size of my fist. Every morning I go into our garden and admire the corn, just as Kishelemukong did so long ago. In the sunniest patch of the garden the corn grows fastest, and a few ears have already been picked and roasted.

We all had a few kernels of roasted new corn as a treat. The tender-sweet corn crunched between my teeth and filled my mouth with juice sweeter than an apple's.

One night it begins to rain hard and doesn't stop all the next day. We sit in our wigwams and stoke our starfires. The rain makes the fires hiss and sputter. Late in the day White Eyes steps outside and puts a rabbit skin over the smoke hole in the roof. Now the smoke has nowhere to go and fills our wigwam. We cough and our eyes sting.

Our village above the cave slowly fills with shallow pools, and the children splash in the water for sport. I volunteer to watch Chickadee splash in one of the pools just to get out of the smoky wigwam. Adults poke anxious faces out of wigwam door flaps to look at the sky.

The woman with the stone pot goes from wigwam to wigwam, carefully filling up the pot with coals from each starfire.

By evening water trickles into the wigwams. The men

quickly dig ditches around our homes to keep more rain from coming in. They dig a long ditch all the way around our village for the same reason. It just rains harder.

We lie awake all night, too tense to sleep. The rain doesn't stop. It's been two nights and one day of hard, steady rain.

At dawn's first light Hepte shakes my shoulder and I sit up. She's holding the two elk collarbones we've used as hoes and shovels. She gives me one of them as she pulls me to my feet.

Our gardens are almost submerged. Just the tops of the pumpkins and squash poke through the water. Everyone begins digging a new ditch around the gardens. We dig faster and faster as the standing water creeps into the ditch. The flat land is saturated, waterlogged from the constant rain. And it's still raining.

At the edges of the gardens cornstalks fall like cut timber into the ditch and are carried away by the swift current. Well-tended vegetable rows turn to mud and flatten out.

All our work! All our food for the winter! Everyone digs faster, but the rain is unrelenting. It just falls faster and faster, too.

I hear the Cuyahoga roaring like a wild thing in the distance.

I remember the stream running through the center of our gardens. That creek must be submerged by now–water running underwater! It reminds me another field full of corn with a stream in the middle of it.

In Connecticut a farmer had dug ditches from a

stream to between his corn rows. The whole town thought he was muddleheaded, but his corn was the best, and the earliest, in Fairfield.

Constance and I had climbed an apple tree to fetch a better look. His ditches looked like a giant water tree lying flat right in the middle of the field, the branches reaching out to water the corn.

I wade to the middle of the garden and look frantically for the stream. It *is* hidden, running under the standing water.

I remember that the cornstalks close to the stream are taller because of the extra water they receive. I find the extra-tall cornstalks and then the place where the new ditch is closest to them. I begin digging a canal from the stream to the new ditch. I push water-clogged mud out with my bare hands. The harder I push, the more muddy water falls into my canal. The elk collarbone shovel works no better. The rain is coming down so hard, it hurts to look up; water rushes into my eyes.

We'll starve without our corn and vegetables. Corn is eaten at every meal. Even the toothless old and young eat a thin porridge of ground corn mixed with water and acorn flour. Corn is our lives. I dig harder and harder.

One entire corner of our garden has been completely swept away. Stalks, leaves, and pumpkins bob aimlessly on the muddy water like the arms, hands, and faces of the drowned.

I dig faster and faster. My elk collarbone shovel breaks in half. I try to use the pieces as a dike around a cornstalk, but they wash away.

I dig with my bare hands again, pushing wet earth out as fast as the water slides in to replace it. My palms and the tips of my fingers begin to bleed. Everything is blurry because of all the water in my face. I pry rocks and stones out of the mud and throw them along the edges of my canal, thinking they might make a barrier. I push against the earth so hard, I slide into the mud again and again.

Coated with mud, my hair is heavy against my neck. More mud slides down my forehead and into my mouth and eyes. I'm crying even though I know that crying won't help us in the least. The last thing we need is more water.

Thunder blasts overhead, so loud I feel it roll through my bones. The sky is a purplish-yellow bruise as lightning tears through the gorge. I smell smoke and see great tongues of fire leaping from tree to tree. How can trees be on fire in this torrential rain?

A mighty westerly wind pulls the flames higher and higher. I sit up in time to see a black funnel cloud on the northern horizon, twisting like a great coiled snake, the tops of burning trees spinning in its wake. The wind whips my muddy hair clear off my shoulders. For one terrifying moment my knees and feet leave the ground.

A tornado.

The twister roars past, but I don't stop digging.

Finally my canal joins the new ditch to the midfield stream. Water rushes past my legs in great swells as the canal fills. As more water flows into the canal, more flows over the cliff, taking bits and pieces of garden with it.

The wind and rain begin to lessen. I hear people shouting for help. Kolachuisen is sitting on the sodden ground, a sobbing lump of muddy misery.

Vegetable rows near the cliff have been swept away, but wonder of wonders, the gardens are beginning to drain. Where there were once submerged vegetable mounds and standing water, there is now saturated soil and the tops of pumpkins and squash poking through the mud. One by one we stop digging.

I straighten up painfully and look around. It's evening; we have been digging without stopping since dawn.

Moonlight shines on the water, the moon's reflection pockmarked by the occasional drop of rain. I see a few stars peeping out between fast-moving clouds. What happened to the burning trees? There are no flames anywhere. The rain must have put the fires out, how many hours ago?

I hold my fingers out and see that they are raw shreds, most of the fingernails gone. My hands drip blood onto the water-clogged ground. Only then do I feel the pain: searing, throbbing, shooting up into my elbows and shoulders. I stumble, whimpering, toward our wigwam with my hands high in the air. Maybe that will keep the blood from gushing out.

"Hepte, Hepte," I scream.

Hepte runs to me and holds my hands up to the moonlight. Blood is running down my arms like sticky ropes of molasses.

"Tonn," she says gently, but I hear the panic and

exhaustion in her voice, "I want to soak your hands in water and herbs, but my cooking pots are full of dry food. I'll have to empty one of the pots. Come with me."

She half carries me the rest of the way. I sit on the summer porch with my back resting against the outside of our wigwam.

"What happened to your elk collarbone?" she asks me.

"Broke, broken. The pain . . ."

"You should have found me. I would have given you a cooking pot to dig with."

White Eyes sits next to me, holding my hands in his. Other people stand around the summer porch looking at my torn fingers.

"Husband, she was digging with her bare hands! Her shovel broke. Our daughter dug more than anyone and with her bare hands," Hepte cries. "I need a bowl, a cooking pot, anything to soak her hands in. Could you find something? Anything?"

"I will look for a bowl," White Eyes says as he jumps off the porch.

A woman I have never spoken to elbows her way to the front of the crowd of people. She looks embarrassed as she hands me my grandmother Campbell's bowl, the one with roses painted on the bottom.

"This is yours," she says, and she quickly steps away.

"My grandmother Campbell's bowl, from Scotland," I say in amazement. In English, too. I'm too tired to think in Unami and too tired to care. "I thought it was gone."

Hepte pushes my hands into the bowl and splashes clear water on them. I groan in agony as they throb and leak blood. She sprinkles some powdered comfrey on my wet fingers and palms. My hands stop bleeding; they begin to tighten and sting. She grinds sodden buckeyes under her heels and adds these to the water. My hands turn cool, then cold, then numb.

I stare at the bowl, glowing bone white in the moonlight. The red roses and green leaves painted on the bottom have turned ash gray and black. The night sky has drained them of color.

Memories flood into my mind, as sharp as lightning, as painful as fire.

I was kneeling in a strawberry patch and holding this very bowl. Under the jagged, dull-green leaves the wild strawberries hid, as shy as deer. My father's cows and sheep were watching me. It was a fresh, beautiful morning in early summer, the sort of day that arches up, up, up, as though it will never end.

But I was too angry and peevish to enjoy that summer morning.

White Eyes comes back and places me in his lap.

"No," I moan in English. "No more, no more."

I was screaming at Ma and Dougal. I said things to my mother, words full of spite and hate. I may never see her again.

"No more." I hold my hands in front of me, as though by blocking my sight I could block the memories, too.

"Tonn," Hepte says, "I know you're in pain, but this is

good medicine." She pushes my hands back into the bowl.

She and White Eyes talk. Their conversation has a floaty, distant quality to it, as though I am hovering overhead.

Grandfather joins us on the summer porch.

"How is she?" I hear him say.

"She was moaning because her hands hurt," Hepte says. "Husband, hold her steady. They should soak longer."

I rest my head on White Eyes' chest, and he gathers me closer. I'm surprised to feel his heart pounding against my ear; he's worried about me.

My torn fingers and palms are numb; even my forearms feel frozen to the elbows. My hands and arms throb with neither heat nor pain.

Hepte, White Eyes, and Grandfather talk softly to one another. I want to ask about Chickadee but I can't put the words together in my head, either in English or in Unami.

Perchance it's the effect of the comfrey and buckeyes, but I have a wondrous feeling of falling off a cliff, just like one of our lost pumpkins. So that's why it's called falling asleep! But I don't remember ever falling asleep this hard or this fast before.

As my eyes close, White Eyes and Hepte's conversion drifts farther away from me as the Campbell memories come closer.

I remember spilling milk from the butter churn and not caring that it was spilled. Lady Grey and her kittens formed a crescent at my feet to lick it up, while behind them the sun was rising red over the Susquehanna. Dougal slept late into the morning.

I especially remember hot, burning rage, just as my tongue burned from eating too many wild strawberries.

Was that angry, bitter little girl picking strawberries really me? What on earth did she know of anger, or sorrow, or hunger, or strength?

The worst part of my captivity is how much I've changed. I'm sure my parents and Dougal think of me and pray for me. How could they not? But if they could see me now, here, this evening–would they know the dark young woman in braids and buckskin sitting in White Eyes' lap? Would they even want to know her? Would they want to know why and how I've changed so much?

Surely the Campbells wouldn't even recognize me. The only clue to who I am is the rose bowl in my lap.

They love the Mary I used to be. I know my childhood is gone, torn away from me (and them) just as surely as the tornado tore away our gardens.

Their life seems strange to me now, too. My mother, shut away in a dark, stuffy cabin instead of enjoying the outdoors. My father, working frantically against time to turn a profit on his claim instead of thinking of the earth as a blessing we all share. My brother, thinking of animals as fur instead of marveling at the living, breathing creature underneath.

The Campbells are gone, Mary. Even if you're rescued and see them again someday, they're still gone. You've changed too much.

"Good-bye," I whisper, and I weep harder than I've wept in years.

I wake up in the middle of the night with my hands bandaged and my stomach starving. I find some cornmeal, and I chew and chew until it's finally mushy enough to swallow. I chew and swallow handful after handful.

Our starfire's embers glow as brightly as ever. Grandfather, Hepte, Chickadee, and White Eyes sleep soundly, their tired faces glowing orange in the firelight.

Very slowly and without making a sound, I creep to the stone water jar near the door flap and drink until I feel the cornmeal beginning to swell in my stomach.

I study their faces. These are the people I think about by day and dream about by night. I'd trust them with my life.

"Good night, Turtle clan," I whisper. I crawl back to my pine needles, roll over, and go to sleep.

The next morning we awake to sunshine and singing birds. We hurry outside before breakfast to look at the damage.

The air is crisp and fresh and there is no wind.

The ditches are full of standing water, as still as mirrors.

About two dozen cornstalks are down. Three boys find another dozen or so at the mouth of the cave far below us; the surging water carried them over the cliff wall. The boys drag the stalks up the cliff trail. Chickadee, Kolachuisen, and the other women and girls replant them in the damp ground.

The pumpkin and squash vines the boys find at the bottom of the cliff are a tangled and shredded mess, the pumpkins and squash all waterlogged and smashed. We have no choice but to bury them as fertilizer for the crops that remain.

Our Three Sisters vegetable rows did all right, considering. Chickadee and Hepte carefully tuck the exposed pumpkin, squash, and bean roots back into the soil. I can't dig. My hands are bandaged in soft strips of deerskin.

My job is to stamp the ground with my feet after the roots have been covered. I stamp and stamp all day. By the time we're finished, my hands throb in pain again.

I work almost as hard today as I did yesterday. Finally all the vegetables that will ever be salvaged have their roots back in the ground, with another month or so before the harvest. All we can do is hope and pray there'll be food for the winter.

We all swim in the river to wash away yesterday's mud. I hold my hands in the air as Hepte scrubs my scalp hard, then rinses and rinses my hair in the river's current.

Hepte soaks my hands again, then unwraps the deerskin strips. My hands look as though the flesh has peeled right off them, with nothing left but bright-red muscle. She rubs the same paste of comfrey and buckeye onto my hands and they turn peculiar again–first tight, then cold, and finally numb.

That evening, as I lie on my bed of pine needles, I marvel at how hard I've worked these last two days. I worked as hard as anyone. I didn't feel sorry for myself or complain about being tired, aching, thirsty, or hungry. I didn't worry about my future and when (or if) I'd be rescued. I was too busy saving our food supply to think about me.

I have scarcely thought about Mary Caroline Campbell, and all her troubles, since the night the rain started. It felt good, not worrying and fussing so much.

And yet now I know I have more strength, courage, and resolve than I would have ever dreamed possible. It's like finding a treasure I didn't know was mine. I know I can face anything.

14

Woman-Who-Saved-the-Corn

IT MUST BE LATE SEPTEMBER. The afternoons have lost their steamy softness, and the mornings and evenings have a dry, cool snap to them. Slanting sunshine pulls our shadows away from us as we work in the gardens. Already I see mist swirl-dancing on the cooling river at sunrise. Hepte says it's the Green Corn Moon.

But I'd call it the Harvest Moon because we're harvesting our crops. For the first time since leaving the Allegheny, we have more than enough to eat. Hepte has been making corn soups mixed with acorn flour and sweetened with wild raspberries. We feast on samp fried in deer fat, which we eat with roasted squirrel and blueberries. We eat corn bread sweetened with honey for breakfast.

The pumpkins and squash are almost ready. These we'll dry in the sun, then save in the storehouse for the long winter. Hepte will add them to winter stewpots of venison and cornmeal.

Maybe next year Mrs. Sequin will give me some apple seeds all the way from Montreal.

I look proudly at our rescued rows of corn, squash, beans, and pumpkins and marvel at how much work went into them. I spent every day this spring and summer working in our garden. We all did–the women, children, and old men–working day after day in the hot sunshine or cool rain. Even Chickadee learned how to swat flies, chase the crows away, and spot and pull weeds.

The vegetable rows extend past the wigwams, the storehouse, and the streambed in straight, orderly lines. The cornstalks glow in the clear autumn sunshine. The pumpkin and squash vines twist between the stalks, their darker-green leaves a pretty contrast to the bright-green corn.

The stalks will lose their color when the solid cold weather comes. Their crackling, butter-yellow husks will be made into cornhusk dolls for the little girls and laid out as soft mattresses for the old people.

The bare ears will be dried and used as kindling. The cornstalk roots will be dried and pounded into powder for winter soups. Children will chew on fresh stalks as a rare treat; the water inside the stalks is as sweet as sugar. No wonder our whole lives revolve around corn.

When my arms are full of ears, I stop to admire the vegetable mounds again. The bright-blue sky has billowy clouds piled high in the west–a storm is coming. The wind feels cool on my face.

Why do I love spending time in our garden? I've never thought of myself as a farmer. But each bright vegetable, each golden ear of corn, fills me with pride and a sense of quiet accomplishment.

My father Campbell would be proud of this garden.

I try to push the thought away, but it's too late. My eyes flood with tears. My chest hurts, my heart weighted down as with a stone.

The Campbells! They seem smaller somehow, diminished; that makes me feel even worse. Time and distance have changed them, too. The Campbells are just people, after all, trying to cull some wheat out of a world too filled with chaff.

I know why captives change over so completely, why I will, little by little, change more and more the longer I stay here. Our hearts yearn to belong. That's why we let go of the past, or at the very least loosen our grip on it.

In the first months of my captivity I often thought about what a torment I was as a daughter and a sister to the Campbells. Always complaining, always aggrieved, always so sure I was getting the worst part of the bargain at every turn. The way I was fills me with shame.

But I was raging at them, too, because I was not the only one in the wrong. Families get set in a pattern, just like a quilt–the Selfish One, the Lazy One, the Favorite, the Martyr, the Tyrant–repeating the same squabbles and misunderstandings again and again.

Life is too precious to waste in such vexing bitterness.

The shame is gone now, as is the rage. What's left is

overwhelming pain, dull eyed and stone cold. But if my grief means I love them, and forgive them, and miss them with all my soul, then surely the Campbells grieve for me too, in the same way and for the same reasons. Until we're all together again, that is my comfort.

My pride reminds me of a family of mice that lived in our Connecticut corncrib. During an especially bitter winter evening, I placed fabric remnants in a snug corner of the crib for their bedding. The next morning every scrap of cloth had been moved to another corner of their choosing.

Even mice want to re-create the world in their image. I know pride's a sin, but why would people be less prideful than mice?

We all want to make our mark on the world. We all want to leave grand evidence of our having been here. Whether it's westering, or growing a garden, or mound building, or not letting the starfires burn out, or even pretending to be an ambassador's wife, we all want to leave a legacy as big as the hills.

Next year we'll have more vegetable mounds, over there, I say to myself, in Unami this time. And over there in that sunny spot I'll plant my apple seeds. I can almost taste the apples crunching between my teeth.

A breeze catches in the cornstalks; the drying stalks rattle a warning of winter's cold. The clouds roll in from the west and block the sun. A cold wind sounds like winter–it roars through the gorge and whispers through the pines. I shiver and I think cozy thoughts about sitting in front of the fire and listening to stories.

Steam from the cookpots drifts past my nose. Every cooking pot we own is bubbling with something delicious–venison stews, corn chowders, berry soups. The wondrous smells make my stomach growl. But it's almost a snug, homey feeling to be so hungry, because I know there's plenty to eat.

Every stewpot is bubbling in my honor.

Tonight is my naming ceremony. From now on, only to myself will I be known as Mary Caroline Campbell.

I wonder what name Grandfather has chosen for me.

As the sun goes down, all two hundred Delaware are waiting for me by the storehouse. All two hundred are smiling at me. The woman who stole my lace collar is smiling. The two brothers who marched with me from the Susquehanna are smiling identical smiles. Even Smallpox Scars, the one who killed Sammy, is smiling and nodding.

Hepte, White Eyes, and Chickadee are next to Grandfather, who is standing in front of our biggest caldron. As I walk toward him, the crowd separates and gives way.

Grandfather hands me a huge turtle shell.

"Drink," he says.

I drink cool water with corn pollen floating on top.

"*Xkwe,*" he says. "Drink again."

While I drink, I run the word over in my mind.

"Schway, schway," I mutter to myself. "That means 'woman.'"

"*Wtaloksin,*" he says. "Drink again."

I sip from the shell. "Wta lok sin," I say to myself. "'Help.' No, 'save.' No . . . 'saved.'"

"*Haskwim,*" Grandfather says. "Drink again."

That's easy. "Corn," I think. Woman-Who-Saved-the-Corn.

That's me!

"'Woman-Who-Saved-the-Corn,' is that right?" I whisper to Grandfather in English. "Is that my new name?"

He puts his finger to his lips and gives me a wink.

We feast all night. I can't remember a time when I was so full, except perhaps a Christmas years ago. My full stomach fills me with sleepy contentment, like a warm blanket but on the inside.

For the first time since the deluge, my hands are completely free of bandages. My stubby, nailless fingers look like burned-down candles. They always hurt at the end of the day, especially if I've been working hard. My palms still look like raw meat, but they're healing. I hide my hands in my sleeves whenever I can.

"Nuxkwis," Grandfather says. He draws my hands out of my sleeves and holds them. "You saved an entire people with these hands. Why do you hide them?"

I rest my hands in my lap.

Drums and turtleshell rattles come out from wigwams, and musicians play and play far into the night. Dancers circle a huge, popping bonfire, their intricate steps lit up in the firelight.

All evening people bring me presents–new buckskin

tunics, beaded jewelry, a beautifully carved spoon of cherry wood. Kolachuisen gives me a corn-husk doll and sits beside me.

I think, Why not? I don't need it anymore. A promise springs from the heart and is savored in the mind. I will see the Campbells again.

"I have something for you," I tell her. I run to our wigwam and come back with the bluebird feather I found last spring.

"Oh!" she cries. "Thank you." Kolachuisen holds the feather in one hand and gives me a hug.

"I'll keep it always," she whispers.

"Tonn," Hepte cries in alarm, "you're not wearing your moccasins. For such a special occasion!"

"They no longer fit. My feet are too big."

Hepte's eyes fill with tears.

"But I want to keep them, always," I say quickly. "I want to remember the daughter who had them before me. Although our feet are no longer the same, perhaps one day our hearts will be."

"Perhaps," Hepte says. When she fills my bowl with another helping of berry soup, her eyes are shining.

"*Gahes,*" I say softly, "thank you."

Afterword

Except for Chickadee, Hepte, and Kolachuisen, everyone in *The Beaded Moccasins* was a real person. Even the Frenchman, François Sequin, had a trading post on the banks of the Cuyahoga River, close to where downtown Cleveland, Ohio, is now.

Mary Campbell, Mary Stewart, and her son Sammy were captured by the Delaware in the summer of 1759, at Penn's Creek, near the banks of the Susquehanna River in Snyder County, Pennsylvania. Sammy Stewart was killed soon after their capture. Mary and Mrs. Stewart were then taken to a Delaware village along the Allegheny River in Armstrong County, in western Pennsylvania.

Mary Campbell was adopted as the granddaughter of Netawatwees Sachem, and was well treated during her captivity.

That same summer the British sent the few Delaware who were still living in the eastern woodlands westward into the Ohio wilderness. Mary Campbell and Mrs. Stewart went with them as their prisoners.

Mary Campbell really did live in a wide, shallow cave above the Cuyahoga River that first winter. That cave, now called the Mary Campbell Cave, is located in Gorge Park in Cuyahoga Falls, Ohio. The following spring the Delaware built a village on flat land near the cave.

Why were Mary and Mrs. Stewart kidnapped in the first place? The tradition of captive taking goes back to prehistoric America. Tribes were eager to replace loved ones lost to warfare and illness. The replacements, if they were willing to be replacements, were treated just as lovingly as the originals.

According to Norman Heard (in *White Into Red: A Study of the Assimilation of White Persons Captured by the Indians*), the assimilation process took approximately five years, and rarely did a child successfully resist it. For girls under twelve years old and boys under fourteen–that is, before puberty–the assimilation process was much faster than for adults.

The rest of the story–Mary's long march, what it felt like to be so far from home, spending a long, cold Ohio winter in a cave, what happened to Mrs. Stewart, what it was like living with people so different from herself–is fiction.

In real life Mary did see the Campbells again.

In 1764 the British ordered all white captives on the western frontier to return to Fort Pitt. In November of that year a Swiss mercenary named Lt. Col. Henry

Bouquet collected captives on the Tuscawaras River and escorted them to the fort. One historian said that on the Tuscawaras, Netawatwees "wept as he handed Mary to the commanding officer."

In the spring of 1765 some 356 captives were reunited with their long lost families at Fort Pitt. Almost six years after her capture, Mary was met by her mother and her brother, Dougal Campbell. There is no evidence that she saw her father again. According .to the records, Mary "showed some reluctance at being returned to her family."

Mary Stewart was reunited with a husband she hadn't seen in six years. She brought with her a four-year-old daughter named Samantha.

Mary went back to Penn's Creek, Pennsylvania, and married a man named Joseph Willford. She had twelve children.

The British signed a treaty with the Delaware and all the other native people of Ohio. No white settlers would be allowed in *if* all white captives were returned.

The British kept their word. Except for missionaries in the mission towns of Schoenbrunn, Salem, and Gnadenhutten, the westward expansion of the frontier stopped at the Ohio River.

In 1778 White Eyes was a sachem in his own right. He was killed by a seventeen-year-old frontiersman named Lewis Wentzel.

In March 1782 American troops led by Col. David Williamson entered the town of Gnadenhutten. They killed over ninety Delaware converts. The first to be killed was an old man named Abraham Netawatwees.

After the Revolutionary War the British lost the Ohio Valley. George Washington himself claimed more than ten thousand acres of prime Ohio River land as American settlers poured into what was then the western wilderness. One of those settlers was Mary's oldest son.

The Delaware, Wyandot, Shawnee, and Miami were pushed west into what is now Indiana.

There is one fascinating bit of evidence about Mary's later years. Neighbors referred to her children as "those Mohawks," so we can only assume she taught them to appreciate Native American culture.

Mary Campbell Willford died in 1801, two years before Ohio was admitted into the Union as the seventeenth state. Her Willford descendants still live in Wayne County, Ohio.

Mary wonders if the mound builders saw the mastodons (the *yah-qua-whee*). We know this would not have been possible. Archeologists have dated mastodon bones to the Paleo-Indian era (23,000-3,000 B.C.). The mound builders lived in the Hopewell era (200 B.C.-A.D 500). The mounds they left still dot the northeastern Ohio countryside, especially near the rivers.

The Delaware do have a story of why they killed the mastodons, and how the mastodons' extinction brought about the cranberry.

There were once twenty tribes among the Delaware.

Mary mentions the Unami, Mohicans, and Munsees. The Wappingers, Esopus, Raritans, Massapequas, Wampanoags, Susquehannas, Catskills, Hackensacks, Rockaways, Nanticokes, Minisinks, Unahachaugs, and Powhatans were also part of the Delaware confederacy.

The Delaware lived in what is now eastern New York State, including New York City and Long Island; eastern Pennsylvania; New Jersey; Delaware; Maryland; and Virginia.

The ancient name of the Delaware is *lanni Lenape,* which means "the People." They changed their name to Delaware more than 350 years ago because of the first governor of Virginia, Baron Thomas West de la Warr.

Today there are few Delaware left. The Stockbridge-Munsee band of Mohicans live in Wisconsin; more Mohicans live in Ontario, Canada. The Unami and other Delaware live in Anadarko, Oklahoma. I'm indebted to The Language Project of the Delaware Tribe of Western Oklahoma for all their help with the Unami words in *The Beaded Moccasins: The Story of Mary Campbell.*

Glossary

Buchahelagas (buck a HEL a gus): Killbuck
chitanisinen (chee tah NEE see nen): strength
Coquetakeghton (coke TA keg ton): White Eyes
Cuyahoga (kye a HOE ga): Crooked River
gahes (ga HEESS): mother
haskwim (ha SKEEM): corn
heh-heh (heh-heh): yes
Hepte (HEP teh): Swan
hoking (HO king): territory
kamis (KA meess): sister
keko windji? (GEH ko WIN jee): why?
Kishelemukong (kih shel MOO kong): the Creator
Kolachuisen (ko la CHEW ee sen): Beautiful Bluebird
ku (coo): no
lappi (la PEE): again
Makiawip (MAHK ee a wip): Red Arrow
makwa (MAHK wah): bear
muxomsa (moo CHUM sa): grandfather
nuxkwis (NUK wiss): grandchild
Netawatwees (neh ta WAT wees): newcomer
sipi (SIP ee): river

Tamaqua (TOM ah kwah): Beaver
Tankawon (TON ka won): Little Cloud
tonn (tawn): daughter
Tuskawaras (tus ka WAR as): Old Town
Wapashuiwi (wap a SHOE wee): White Lynx
wtaloksin (wta LOK sin): saved
xkwe (shway): woman
yah-qua-whee (YAH kwah wee): mastodon

Sources

Demos, John. *The Unredeemed Captive.* New York: Knopf, 1994.

Eckert, Allan W. *That Dark and Bloody River: Chronicles of the Ohio River Valley.* New York: Bantam, 1995.

Grumet, Robert S. *The Lenapes.* Frank W. Porter III, ed. New York: Chelsea House, 1989.

Hawke, David Freeman. *Everyday Life in Early America.* New York: Harper, 1989.

Heard, J. Norman. *White Into Red: A Study of the Assimilation of White Persons Captured by Indians.* Metuchen, N.J.: Scarecrow, 1973.

Heckewelder, Reverend John. *Narrative of the Mission of the United Brethren Among the Delaware and Mohegan*

Indians. Reprint: New York: Arno and The New York Times, 1971.

"Hopewell, Prehistoric America's Golden Age," from *Early Man*, Winter 1979. Reprint: Chillicothe, Ohio: Craftsman Printing, 1990.

The Language Project, Delaware Tribe of Western Oklahoma. Anadarko, Oklahoma.

McCutchen, David. *The Red Record: The Wallam Olum: The Oldest Native North American History.* Garden City Park, NY: Avery, 1993.

McPherson, J. Beverly. "Mary Campbell, the First White Child on the Western Reserve." Paper given to the Cuyahoga Falls Chapter of the Daughters of the American Revolution, 1934. Akron Public Library archives.

National Archives. *Revolutionary War Pension and Bounty-and-Warrant Application Files.*

Saguin, Marilyn. "The Legend of Mary Campbell." *Our Town Magazine, The Akron Beacon Journal*, December 1985.

Schumacher, Fred, Head Librarian, Cleveland Metroparks Zoo.

Smithsonian Bureau of Ethnology. *Guide to North*

American Indian Tribes. Washington, D.C.: Smithsonian Press, 1979.

Taylor Memorial Library, Cuyahoga Falls, Ohio. "The Mary Campbell Papers."

Weslager, C. A. *The Delaware Indians: A History.* New Brunswick, N.J.: Rutgers University Press, 1972.